Matt Shaw Publications

ISBN: 97982761
Imprint: Independentl

The characters in this book are purely fictitious.

Any likeness to persons living or dead is purely coincidental.

THE WHITE ROOM RUNS RED

MATT SHAW

Part One
The White Room

Chapter One

He watched from across the room. She was sleeping soundly; quiet little snores which brought him some comfort despite his predicament. *Naked*, just as he was.

It took everything not to call across and wake her. The only reason he didn't was that, with her sleeping, he was safe from whatever *this* was. Was she a part of it? Was she the one who, somehow, had brought him to this room? Was she the one who had removed his clothes and hidden them? No. Ridiculous. It couldn't have been her. At least, certainly not by herself.

She was in her thirties. A pretty woman; blonde hair, and a slight frame. As she was lying on the other single bed in the white room, he could only guess her height. Five foot five? He was bulky, muscular. Six foot two. There was no way she could have brought him to this place by herself. But then, if she had an accomplice, how come there was no one else in here?

She started to stir. His heart skipped a beat. *This is it*. Her eyes opened and immediately squinted against the harsh fluorescent lights. Only once comfortable to do so did they open fully and -

- *immediate* panic.

She sat bolt upright and let out an audible gasp when her crystal blue eyes fixed upon him. Understandably scared, she pushed herself up against the corner of the room with a desperate plea, 'Don't hurt me.' Her voice was sweet, almost exactly as he'd imagined she'd sound. He was wrong about the colour of her eyes though. He thought they'd be green, maybe even hazel.

'My name is James,' he said. He could tell from her face, the way her eyes darted around the white room, that she wasn't hearing a single word he said. It didn't matter. He carried on speaking in that hope that she'd hear *something* at least. 'From your reaction, I take it you don't know how we came to be here?'

The pair were in a small room, approximately twelve by ten. In one corner of the room there was a white toilet with no lid to the white seat. Across one wall, his bed. Across the other, her bed. A single, harsh fluorescent light strip was imbedded in the high ceiling. A single, large mirror stretching from one wall to the other. There was a door directly opposite the mirror; it had no handle, nor a lock yet - when James had tried it - it wouldn't budge.

She noticed the door and ran towards it, pushing against it with all her weight.

'It's locked,' James said. 'I've already tried that.'

She didn't care. She tried digging her nails into the cracks between door and wall, hoping to prize it open but - still - it wouldn't give.

James got up from his bed. 'You're going to hurt yourself,' he said as she immediately backed herself into the far corner, as far away from him as the room would allow. He backed up, not wishing to scare her further. He continued, 'The last thing I recall was being at work.' James said, 'I work in an office block in the financial side of town.' The more details he gave her, the more he hoped she realised he wasn't a threat. 'Business as usual, dealing with my clients and balancing books of the wealthy.'

'Someone help me! Is anyone out there?!' She was screaming loud enough to be heard *if* there was anyone out there but,

'I don't think there's anyone out there,' he said. 'I've been awake for a while now and no one has come to see me.' Hoping he could calm her down enough to try and figure this out together, he asked, 'What's your name?'

She hesitated a moment before, 'Emily.'

'Hello, Emily. I'm James.' He asked his original question again, 'I take it you don't know how you came to be here either?'

Emily shook her head. A white tear ran down her cheek. She wiped it away, presuming the colour was nothing more than a reflection from the harsh white walls. 'Where are my clothes?'

'I don't know where *our* clothes are,' James admitted. 'What was the last thing you remember before waking up?'

'I was in my car.' Another wave of panic washed over her. 'I was going to the school to pick my daughter up. Where's my daughter? Is she okay?'

'I'm sorry. I don't know.' Gesturing around the room, he said, 'This is all I know…'

Emily broke down. What started with one tear spilling from her left eye and running down her cheek turned to many. All of them *white.* James watched on awkwardly, unsure whether he was meant to go over and try and comfort her or whether such a move would only serve to make things worse. He presumed the latter. When Emily wiped the tears away, she noticed their colouration. 'And what the fuck is this?'

James didn't know. 'Maybe a side effect to whatever they used to get us here? But I don't know.' He pointed to a bruise on his arm. 'Do you have a mark on your arm?' In the centre of it, there was a small pin-hole from where *something* had been injected.

Emily looked at her arm and, sure enough, she had a similar mark. 'Why is this even happening?'

'I'm sorry but I really don't know. I'm in the exact same position as you. I don't know how I got here, I don't know *why* I'm here. Outside, in the real world, I'm a nobody. An anonymous voice on the other end of the phone, helping clients. I go home to an empty house, hardly have any friends that I see. Most of my nights I'm either reading books, watching films or playing on my PC. I'm a literal *nobody.*' Saying the words out loud hurt; lonely, depressed thoughts often in his mind but never spoken and certainly not to someone he'd only just met. He tried to push the thoughts back down where they were normally buried and changed the subject, 'What about you?'

Emily was still trying to get her crying under control. 'About me, what?'

'Are you a *somebody*? Would anyone have any reason to… Put you here?'

'I'm a single mum. I have a six year old daughter and a part-time job in a newsagent close to my house. I'm… just me.' She looked around the room and said, 'I don't belong here.'

None of this made sense. James knew he was telling the truth and could only *hope* she was too. If she was then, they were two nobodies with no connection to one another and no business being locked in a place like this.

'So what are we supposed to do now?' Emily's question was fair but not one which could be answered. Knowing this, Emily didn't wait for an answer and, instead, asked a second question. 'Do you think we're being watched?' She was looking at the mirror. She'd seen enough true crime documentaries; criminals being interviewed in small rooms while other members of law enforcement watched through a special two-way mirror.

Despite having more time to think about their predicament, James hadn't stopped to consider this possibility. He got up and walked over to the mirror, pressing his forehead against it to see if there was any kind of visible movement on the other side. If there was anyone watching, he couldn't see them.

'There's a test you can do,' Emily said. She crossed the room, leaving a little distance between her and James. He stood back and watched as she put her finger to the mirror. 'If it's a normal mirror, there'll be a little gap between your nail and its reflection,' she explained. 'Having no gap suggests it's a two-way mirror.'

'And?'

There was no gap.

Chapter Two

A hollow sound reverberated through the room when they pounded their fists against the mirror; another sign that there was *something* behind it. Both Emily and James were shouting. *Is there anyone in there? What do you want? Let us out.* The same phrases over and over again with no forthcoming answers.

James was the first to step away from the mirror, returning to his bed where he sat on the edge of the mattress. 'Maybe they're on a break,' he said. 'Or maybe there's no one there? Or, perhaps, it's just a mirror.'

'It's not. It's a two-way mirror. I know it is. Someone's on the other side, watching us.' One more blow against the mirror. She stepped away and cast another eye around the room. 'Is there anything we can use?'

'Use?'

'To break it. I'm telling you; it's a two-way mirror.' She slammed her fist against the mirror again. It was clear she wasn't about to break it using only her hands. Even if she could have, it wouldn't happen without significant damage to them. 'There must be something we can use.' She cast her eyes around the room. The beds were bolted to the floor, as was the one toilet in the room. She sighed and hit the mirror again before going back over to her own bed. 'So, what are we supposed to do?'

James shrugged. 'What *can* we do?'

'Welcome.' A voice, masculine, came through a hidden speaker startling both Emily and James in the process. They both stood.

'Hello? Who is this? Where are we?'

Emily was more direct. 'Let us out of here!'

The voice spoke again, 'Freedom comes at the end of the experiment.'

'Experiment?' James asked, '*What* experiment?'

'You are both here as part of an experiment. That is all you need to know for now.' The voice continued, 'While you stay with us, we hope to make you both as comfortable as possible, but such comfort is only given with your full cooperation.'

'What do you mean?'

'At various times, our team will come in to monitor your vitals. Before their arrival, the lights in the room will turn red. When this occurs, you must stand on opposite sides of the room, facing the wall with your backs to the door. You cannot turn around unless instructed to do so. Our team will check your blood pressure and your temperature. Occasionally, when necessary, they will draw some blood which will also be analysed. On each visit, they will leave you with a menu card.'

'A menu card?'

'On this menu there will be a meal choices for the following day. Chicken, steaks, burgers, vegetarian options if preferred; all dietary considerations catered for. Today we have chosen the meals for you but trust they will be to your liking.'

'Just let us out,' Emily screamed. 'I have a daughter!'

As stated, behave and you can be very comfortable here. A word of warning though: If you try and break free, if you try and hurt our staff, your meals will be limited to the bare minimum; a bland diet of water, rice, bread, porridge. There'll be enough sustenance to keep you going but no luxuries and no entertainment to keep you amused and your minds active moving forward. I am sure you have already noticed there's not much in there for you. It feels like a prison. But this can all change so long as you play your part accordingly.'

James muttered, 'This is fucking ridiculous. It has to be a joke.' The problem was, he didn't know anyone who'd go to such lengths for "a joke". It also wasn't funny. Also, if it *had been* a joke, why would he be put somewhere with a random person he didn't know and seemingly had nothing in common with?

The voice ignored him. 'Our staff will be along shortly. Today they will not be taking any blood; only leaving you a menu card and checking the aforementioned vitals. Remember: Do as instructed, play nice and be rewarded. You will only ever be punished if you try and hurt our staff or make further attempts to escape the room. Once the experiment is over, you will be freed.'

Her thoughts fixated on her daughter, Emily wanted to know, 'How long is the experiment? How long do we have to be here? And what about my daughter?' For all she knew, someone could have snatched her daughter from school, and she was locked in another room somewhere, scared and crying for her mum. The voice didn't answer. 'Hello?' Still nothing. She called out louder this time, 'HELLO?'

'I think they've gone,' James said, stating the obvious.

Emily knew they were still there though, even if they had stopped talking. The two-way mirror there? They'd always be watching. 'What are we supposed to do now?'

James shrugged. 'I guess we wait.'

'For *what*?'

He didn't have an answer. At least, none which would give her any comfort.

'I feel sick,' Emily said. It could have been the nerves and anxiety, or it could have been whatever they'd used to knock her out and bring her to the room.

'We just need to stay calm,' James said. 'You heard him, when this is over we're free. We just need to focus on that.' Easier said than done; James didn't have a child at home. He didn't even have a pet. As a mother, all Emily could think about was her daughter. For a moment, they both sat in silence. It was interrupted when the light's room turned to a dark shade of red. *Someone* was about to enter the room.

Not wishing to fall foul of the given instructions at the first hurdle, James was the first to move to his corner of the room. As per the commands given, he stood in the corner with his back to the door. Emily hesitated a moment before she too did the same.

The door opened.

Chapter Three

Trolley wheels audibly squeaked as a medical trolley was pushed into the room. Both Emily and James were desperate to turn around, to face whoever had come in, but both kept to the given instructions, *Do not move until instructed to do so.*

For Emily, she just wanted to see if she recognised the person. If she did, at least she would be able to try and work out why she was trapped there.

James's thoughts were somewhat darker, wondering if he could take them down so as to try and break free from whatever this was. The biggest thing holding him back being that whoever arranged this would surely have taken such a move into consideration *and* have a means to stop it. In his mind's eye, he pictured a tank of a man standing behind him. He was surprised when it was a female voice which spoke out, 'I'm just going to put this sleeve around your arm.' He didn't have a chance to react before she did as warned and put the sleeve to the blood pressure machine around his bicep. 'Okay you're going to feel it getting tighter.' A few audible button presses, and the sleeve did indeed tighten. She removed it from his arm with a, 'Thank you.'

From the sound of the voice, she sounded sweet and almost innocent in her demeanour which only served to confuse him further. What was someone like that doing in a place like this?

'If you can turn to face me,' she said.

James didn't hesitate. He turned around and was shocked to see a petit woman standing there with a thermometer in her hand. To go with the nurse's uniform she was wearing, she had a medical mask covering the tip of her nose and her mouth. From what he could see of her face though - she looked young; barely qualified from whatever college she had studied at and with the biggest puppy dog eyes he'd ever seen. She looked like butter wouldn't melt. 'Why are we here?'

'I just need to put this under your tongue.' She held the thermometer up to his face. James opened his mouth and raised his tongue. She slid the probe in, and he closed his mouth around it. A few seconds later, the device in her hand beeped having recorded his temperature. 'Okay, perfect.' Sliding the probe from his mouth, she said, 'Thank you.' She put the tip of the probe into a medical waste bin which hung off the edge of the trolley before installing a new one, ready for Emily's temperature.

James watched as she then jotted down the stats on a clipboard, also resting on the top of the trolley. 'Can you please let us know why we are here? What this experiment is?'

'Thank you. That's it for now. Please turn to face the wall.'

James hesitated a moment, unsure if he was able to push her a little further into talking to him. He decided against it and turned to face the wall.

The nurse made her way across the room, towards Emily, pushing the trolley out in front of her as she did so. The wheels still squeaking as they turned. 'Okay I'm just going to put this sleeve around your arm for your blood pressure.'

Unlike James, Emily followed all given instructions in silence. If the woman wasn't about to open up to him, she wouldn't suddenly change her mind and open up to her. Like James she was also surprised by the nurse's youthful appearance, and, like James, she didn't recognise her.

When the nurse was done, she said, 'Okay if you can please turn and face the wall again.' When Emily did as she was told, the nurse continued, 'I will put your menus on your beds. Take a look at them and, when you've chosen your meals for tomorrow, you can call your choices through the mirror. Your next meal will be with you shortly.' As an aside, she added, 'I hope you have a pleasant stay with us.'

'A pleasant stay? How are we supposed to have a pleasant stay when we don't know where the fuck we are or why we're here? An experiment? Neither of us have signed up for a fucking experiment,' James continued, 'and she has a daughter waiting for her! Can you please just tell us what the hell this is all about? How did we even get here and why the fuck are her tears *white*?'

The nurse said nothing. Pushing the trolley out in front of her, she quietly left the room. The moment the door closed, the lights turned from red back to the bright obnoxious white light both James and Emily had awoken to.

Still irritated, James said, 'This is fucking ridiculous.'

They turned around. Their eyes were immediately drawn to the laminated menus on their beds. After a brief pause, Emily asked, 'Should we have a look?'

James walked over to his bed and picked the menu up. He presumed it would be like a typical hospital menu; plastic food that was easy to heat up in microwaves. He was surprised to notice high quality items with two in particular standing out, steak and lobster. A surprise, yes, but it didn't make any of this feel more acceptable.

Emily said nothing as she looked at the menu.

James watched her face looking for some kind of reaction but there was nothing. If anything, she looked as though she'd entirely shut down. Perhaps the shock of the situation had set in. 'Are you okay?'

Emily laughed. He'd not cracked a joke; it was just a ridiculous thing to ask given the circumstances. She didn't bother to answer. She tossed the menu to the side. 'I'd rather starve than play their games.'

James couldn't help but show his concern. 'I don't think that's a good idea. For one, it's not a pleasant way to die but also, if you don't do as they say, they've already made it clear there will be punishments. Could be for you and you alone or could impact both of us? But even if you don't care about any of that - we need to keep our strength up for whatever comes next. We'll be good for nothing if we starve ourselves…'

'I don't care.'

'You don't care about getting out of here to see your daughter again?' It was a cruel blow, but one James felt was necessary. 'We need to be in this together and we need to be smart about how we handle this. Starving ourselves isn't smart and certainly won't make this a smooth journey into getting released. Unless that is, you *don't* want to see your daughter again?'

Emily snapped, 'Of course I do.'

'Then make smart choices.'

'They need to tell us what is going on!'

'And maybe they will. But all the time we're disobeying them; they won't do *anything* for us. Anyway, there's no point me lecturing you. You're your own person and can make your own mind up…'

'And for all I know, you're a part of all this,' Emily said coldly. James looked at her. He was at a complete loss as to what to say so - said nothing. Instead, he approached the mirror, ready to put in his order.

Chapter Four

The red lights were a welcome break to the brightness of the usual white; James and Emily just wished they'd stay on for longer. No sooner had the staff dropped their meals in and left the room had the lights switched back to the usual, uncomfortable white, signalling that both prisoners were free to leave their respective corners.

The staff had brought in two trays, on which were the couple's first meal in the box room: battered cod, fries and garden peas. In fairness it didn't look a bad meal given the usual standard of "hospital" food they were expecting. Even so, Emily wasn't about to eat it. She'd meant what she'd said, she would rather starve.

James ate. The first few mouthfuls were tentative, unsure as to whether the food had been laced with anything. If it had been *altered,* the extra ingredient was tasteless. 'I think it's okay,' he said, hoping his words - along with the smell of the food - would encourage Emily to give it a try. He was still worried that her refusal to eat anything would have repercussions on how they (whoever "they" were) treated him.

Emily picked the tray up, carried it over to by the door and placed it down on the floor before returning to her bed. She sat without saying a word.

'You still think I work for them, don't you? That I'm a part of all this.' Since sharing her doubt, Emily had been giving James the silent treatment. He'd tried to talk to her, tried reassuring her but she wouldn't even look at him; she just stuck to her corner of the room and stared at the mirror with a look of defiance in her eyes. Normally he wouldn't have cared if someone wanted to talk to him or not but, in this situation, he viewed Emily as his only friend. Whatever this was, they were in it together and while it wouldn't have helped fix anything, it would have been better to have at least one ally to go through this with him. Being given the cold shoulder just made the situation that little more unbearable. 'What can I do to make you trust me?' He added, 'We're in this together. Surely it would be better if we stuck together?' Silence. 'There must be something I can do?'

'You can get me out of here,' she said, finally breaking the silence even if her demand wasn't exactly straight forward.

'I don't know how.'

'All I know is, you seem keen to do as they say and just as keen to try and get me to do the same. For someone who says they don't know what is going on, you seem to be at ease with all of this.'

'At ease? I couldn't be more uncomfortable but what am I supposed to do? Am I supposed to pace the room and shout? What's that going to do other than freak you out? They won't care if I'm in here shouting the odds. For all we know, the room is sound-proof, and they have a button, or something, to press when they *do* want to hear us. The rest of the time, they're watching us in silence. Or am I meant to start thumping the walls hoping that, suddenly, I have developed super-human strength and can punch through what looks like solid brick?' She said nothing. 'Okay, fine. Fuck it.' He picked his tray up and launched it across the room into the mirror. The tray and all its contents fell to the floor with a loud crash but didn't so much as mark the mirror. He screamed at the top of his lungs, 'Let us out, you motherfuckers!' Not done yet, he grabbed Emily's tray from the floor and launched that too. It also fell to the floor, spreading the debris in all directions. He paused, waiting for a response from beyond the mirror. When it was obvious none was coming, he turned to Emily and asked, 'Is that better?'

Emily didn't know what to say. He'd put a show on, that was for sure, but for all she knew it could have all been pre-arranged before today; something for him to do to try and show he was as much as a prisoner as she was.

James walked back to his bed and sat. 'Okay then, ask yourself this, *why* would I be put in here too? What use could I possibly be to them in here? It doesn't make sense.'

'They could have put you in here to ensure I do as they say,' Emily said. 'That I don't spend all my time trying to break free or fight them.'

James laughed, more out of frustration than because he found the situation to be amusing. 'Well then, I don't know what else to say.'

'Then perhaps "say nothing"?'

'Fine. Whatever.'

He repositioned himself on the bed, putting his feet up and leaning back against the wall. Aware he was still naked; he took his pillow and put it over his genitals. There was nothing else to do but wait to hear from those in-charge. He just hoped they wouldn't keep them waiting too long.

* * * * *

BEFORE

'I'm very sorry for the delay, I've been off work sick, but I can assure you, I will have the report over to you before the end of the day,' James said. He was sitting in his office, talking to one of his more demanding customers on the phone.

For the past three months, James had been working on his client's accounts. They had been due the previous week but, due to being off work, he'd not had them finished in time. The client didn't have to give them over to the tax man for another five months but was panicking as to whether he had enough funds in his account to cover the impending payment. By getting the accounts back sooner, it gave him time to "react" if the money owed was more than he'd initially planned and, given he was told the date he'd have said accounts back by, he was understandably annoyed. 'By the end of the day?'

'I assure you; they will be in your emails by this evening - yes,' James confirmed.

'Fine. Because if not I'll just have to take my business elsewhere,' the client said. With how aggressive he could get over the phone, James wouldn't have cared if he had lost the account. His bosses, on the other hand, wouldn't have been so pleased to lose it.

'It won't come down to that.'

'Just don't see why someone else couldn't have stepped in if they knew you were going to be off for a few days.' Most of the businesses' clients thought in a similar way; they were the only customer who needed their books to be balanced. Even those who understood that they were just one client of many, believed themselves to be more important than any of the others within the system. It was a thankless job, especially when the figures *did* come in higher than what the other person had been expecting or when certain expenses were refused.

James tried to explain, 'By the time someone else could have got up to speed with the books, I would have been back.' What made the conversation more frustrating was that James had been off *sick*. It wasn't like he was at home with his feet up, shirking his responsibilities or that he was somewhere exotic, paddling in crystal clear waters. He couldn't even remember the last time he'd taken a proper holiday. But, as ever, he was the bad guy.

'Whatever. If you could just please get me the file by the end of the day…' That was where the conversation ended. There were no goodbyes and no well-wishes for a nice day. The call was simply dropped.

James sighed and put the phone back on its cradle before rubbing his aching chest. Clearly he wasn't quite as "fighting fit" as he had thought he was when he first decided to come back to work, not that he'd make such an admission to the client. It's not like they would have cared. He turned his attention back to the screen; the very same client's report was already loaded up on his screen and, feeling particularly spiteful, he couldn't help but wonder whether he'd be able to get away with deleting some of the expenses to give the ungrateful asshole a bigger bill to pay the HMRC. *Not worth it.* If he tried it and was caught, it would only be his head on the block.

There was a knock on his office door. It opened and his superior, Mark Jacobs, walked in. 'Saw you were back,' he said. 'How are you feeling?' James knew better than to think it was a genuine question. Mark wouldn't have come in to check on his health, it was simply a "polite" opening before he jumped to the *real* reason why he'd come down to his office. 'Had a complaint while you were away.'

'Oh?'

'Mr. Ritchie was chasing his accounts. Apparently they were due last week, and he really needs them,' Mark continued.

'I've literally just got off the phone with him.'

'And?'

James pointed to the screen, turning his laptop round so Mark could see it more clearly. 'He'll have them by the end of the day.'

'That's what we like to know. Just, next time, if you have anything due - let us know so we can step in. Save upsetting the clients.'

'Will do.' James knew there was no point in saying anything else. Mark was aware it would have taken someone else too long to go through the books and get it back in time but there'd been a complaint so "something" had to be said, even if it was bullshit for the sake of sound like he was in charge.

'Anyway, good to have you back,' and, with that, Mark left.

James turned his computer back towards him and sat back in his chair. There was still a fair amount of work to do and if he wanted to get it turned around in time, it was clearly going to be a long day with no breaks. Bad enough on any other day but worse now with the tightness in his chest. He muttered, 'Should have stayed home.'

* * * * *

Unable to keep the thought to himself, and knowing Emily would have thought him mad, James couldn't help but speak it out loud, 'What if we're dead?'

Chapter Five

No one knew what happened when a life ended. There's a lot of speculation with people believing various scenarios but none of them came with any proof. Even those who'd died for a few minutes come back with stories contradicting one another. Some spoke of there being *nothing* on the other side, others spoke of seeing relatives long since deceased and then there were those who talked of seeing a white light. Of all the things said to them, the "white light" was what stuck in James's head. 'What if we're dead?'

'What are you talking about?'

'The white light at the end of the tunnel. What if *this* is what's waiting at the end of that tunnel? What if we're here waiting for judgement or something? That's what this experiment is all about; to see if we're good people?'

Emily frowned. She glanced over to James. He wasn't even looking at her. He was staring at the wall with a faraway look on his face, pillow still covering his modesty. She hesitated a moment before she said, 'You're being serious, aren't you?'

James shrugged. 'It's an explanation.'

'Then why would they come and take our vitals? Why would they offer us meals? If we're dead, we have no vitals *to* take. If we're dead, we wouldn't need to eat.'

'Maybe it's a transitional thing to help us slowly come to terms with what happened.'

'So…' Emily glanced around the room. 'What's this? Cut backs so we don't get our own space now? We have to share with someone we don't know?'

James knew it was a stupid thought for exactly the reasons Emily brought up but at least it was an *explanation*. Despite knowing it was ridiculous, he couldn't shift the feeling though; more so given, other than being trapped in a room, he felt well in himself. A far cry from how he'd been feeling up until waking here.

Emily said, 'We're not dead.' Her tone suggested that, despite her earlier disbelief, she was trying to convince herself more than James. 'I was feeling fine. I took my daughter to school, went about my day -was just a normal day - and was on my way to collect her. I didn't feel unwell.' She said again, 'I'm not dead.'

James got up from his bed. The pillow fell to the floor. He walked over to the mirror and hit the side of his fist against it as he called through, 'Can you tell us what is going on? What are we doing here? What's this experiment? You want us to toe the line and do as we're told but - it would be easier if we knew what the hell was going on!' Behind him Emily leaned down and grabbed a broken shard of the ceramic plate. James saw via the mirror and turned to see what she was doing just as she put it to her wrist. 'What are you doing?'

'If we're dead, this won't do anything. Can't die twice.'

'You said yourself we're *not*,' James said, even though she'd not sounded entirely convinced. 'What then?'

Emily shrugged. 'What does it matter?'

'I'm pretty sure it will matter to your daughter,' he said.

'They'll come in and help me,' she continued, still with a certain level of uncertainty in her voice.

'Will they though? We don't even know who they are. Are you that keen to put your confidence in someone you don't know?'

'They're checking our vitals. Clearly they care.'

James tried to make it clear, 'This isn't a good idea.' Playing the only card, he knew he had, he said again, 'Think of your daughter.'

Emily hesitated a moment. James watched as a thought hit, giving her a true lightbulb moment. Without saying anything, she turned the pointed end of the shard towards James.

James instinctively took a step back. 'What are you doing?'

'You already said you don't have anyone waiting for you at home. What's to stop me from sticking this in you? If they come and help, great. If they don't, what does it matter?'

'You're not going to stab me.' She could try but, if she did, James would have no hesitation in defending himself; consequences be damned.

'At least we'd know the truth though.'

James grabbed a shard of his own. He didn't point it defensively towards his room-mate. Instead, he ran it across his palm. He winced in pain as Emily watched on, both confused and curious. The shard cut his flesh open, and it immediately started to seep a thick, white liquid. Shocked, he dropped the shard to the floor where it broke in two just as the room's lights turned from white to red.

A voice came through the hidden speakers, sterner than the times it had spoken before, 'Please move immediately to your respective corners!'

Neither Emily nor James moved from their spot, although James did turn to the mirror. He raised his hand for them to see the self-inflicted damage and yelled, 'What the fuck is this shit?'

The voice said again, 'Please move to your corners of the room. *Now.*' The volume was slightly increased from the last given instruction.

'Fuck this. Tell us what the fuck is going on!' Mocking the mystery person's voice, James sarcastically added, '*Now.*'

Behind him, the door opened, and two armed guards stormed into the room…

Part Two
Take 2

Chapter Six

She watched from across the room. He was snoring on the other side of it, curled up on his own bed and just as naked. She didn't wake him. She didn't dare. At least with him sleeping, he wasn't touching her; something her panicked mind had already envisioned when she first woke and found herself trapped in the room with him. One step further, she even touched a gentle hand between her legs to feel if there were any signs of soreness from where she'd already been penetrated without consent. To her relief, everything felt as it should but then, a part of her had already told her she wouldn't need to touch herself there to know if she'd been violated. She would have felt sore regardless, and not just necessarily in the one place.

The room was bare. There were two beds, one either side of the room. There was a toilet in the corner too but with no privacy screens to shield them from being watched by the other person, should they have the need to go. There was a handleless door and, along the length of one of the walls, a mirror. She was already pretty sure it was a two-way mirror but, fearful of disturbing *him*, she hadn't got up to investigate, using a method she'd learned from the many True Crime documentaries she'd seen on the various streaming services she was subscribed to. *Put your thumb nail against it; if there's no gap between nail and reflection, it's likely a two-way mirror*. Other than those items, and a strong smell of bleach from where someone had clearly done a very deep clean, there was nothing else in the brightly lit room.

Her thoughts were distracted when, across the room, the man suddenly sat bolt upright with a panicked look of horror in his wide eyes. 'Where the fuck am I?' He turned and saw the woman watching him. 'Who the fuck are you?' She'd instinctively tried to make herself smaller by pushing herself back into the corner where her bed met the wall.

While his reaction was aggressive, it at least showed her that he was very much in the same position as her. Had she woken up second, there was no way she wouldn't have believed he'd not been a part of whatever plan brought her here. In an effort to calm him, she said, 'I don't know how we got here. My name is Emily. I woke up a little while ago in the same position…'

He realised he was naked and quickly grabbed the pillow. He put it over his crotch. 'Where are my clothes?'

'I don't know where *our* clothes are,' she said. She was already hugging herself, hiding her body behind her own pillow as best as she could. She asked, 'What's your name?'

'James,' he said.

On the off-chance she'd not heard her first introduction, she said, 'My name is Emily.'

'Well, *Emily*, do you have any idea where we are?'

'No.'

James got up and walked over to the door. She watched as he tried to force it open but, after less than a minute, it was clear it was stuck fast. He turned back to the mirror and called through, 'Anyone out there?'

Emily said, 'I think it is a two way mirror. There's a method you can use to see if it is.'

'Yeah, I can smash the fucking thing and grab whoever is on the other side.' He started looking around the room. The bed was bolted to the floor; the toilet was clearly not going about to be lifted either. Other than that, there was nothing else which could be used as a "brick". James turned back to the mirror and punched it. All he did was hurt his hand.

'It might just be a wall on the other side.'

'There's no reason why there'd have a mirror in here unless it was to watch us from the other side.'

Emily explained, 'Well if you put your thumb nail up to it… If there's no gap then, chances are, it's two-way.'

James put his hand up against the glass, specifically his thumb.

'Is there a gap?'

'No.' He glared at his own reflection trying to see through both that and the mirror itself, not that he could.

Emily got up and walked over to the mirror. She tried to peer through too but to no avail. She knocked on it; a hollow sound, further proof there was a viewing room on the other end. She knocked on it only to jump back when a voice answered, 'Welcome.'

'Hello? Who is this? Where are we?'

Emily was more direct. 'Let us out of here!'

The voice spoke again, 'Freedom comes at the end of the experiment.'

'Experiment?' James asked, '*What* experiment?' A question which was on Emily's lips too, ready to be asked if he hadn't.

'You are both here as part of an experiment. That is all you need to know for now.' The voice continued, 'While you stay with us, we hope to make you both as comfortable as possible, but such comfort is only given with your full cooperation. At various times, our team will come in to monitor your vitals. Before their arrival, the lights in the room will turn red. When this occurs you must stand on opposite sides of the room, facing the wall with your backs to the door. You cannot turn around unless instructed to do so. Our team will check your blood pressure and your temperature. Occasionally, when necessary, they will draw some blood which will also be analysed. On each visit, they will leave you with a menu card.'

'A menu card?'

'On this menu will be a meal choices for the following day. Chicken, steaks, burgers, vegetarian options if preferred; all dietary considerations catered for. Today we have chosen the meals for you but trust they will be to your liking. As stated, behave and you can be very comfortable here. A word of warning though: If you try and break free, if you try and hurt our staff, your meals will be limited to the bare minimum; a bland diet of water, rice, bread, porridge. There'll be enough sustenance to keep you going but no luxuries and no entertainment to keep you amused and your minds active moving forward. I am sure you have already noticed there's not much in there for you. It feels like a prison. But this can all change so long as you play your part accordingly.'

Emily called through the mirror, 'I have a daughter. I need to get home to my daughter.'

The voice ignored her and continued, 'Our staff will be along shortly. Today they will not be taking any blood; only leaving you a menu card and checking the aforementioned vitals. Remember: Do as instructed, play nice and be rewarded. You will only ever be punished if you try and hurt our staff or make any attempts to escape the room. Once the experiment is over, you will be freed.'

Emily said again, 'When? When will the experiment be over? I need to get home to my daughter!'

The voice said, 'Your daughter is doing fine.'

'What's that supposed to mean? Is she here?' Emily started to panic, picturing her daughter waking to find herself in a room similar to this once. 'Where is she?'

The voice stopped answering.

Having seen Emily get a reaction when she knocked, James tried too. He paused, waiting to hear the voice once again. They stood in silence for minutes, which felt more like hours. 'Now what?'

Chapter Seven

With an audible click, the room's harsh light turned from white to red; the signal that someone was about to enter. Neither James nor Emily moved immediately and, instead, both turned to face the door.

'When the light turns red, you must stand on opposite sides of the room and face the wall with your backs to the door. You cannot turn around unless instructed to do so,' the voice said, coming through the speaker once again.

Emily was the first to move. She walked to the corner closest to her bed and stood there with her back to the door as instructed.

James hesitated. While Emily clearly had a reason - her daughter - to do as she was told, James believed they had nothing to hold over him to ensure he played their game. She had a kid waiting for her at home, he had no one.

'This is your first warning,' the voice said. 'Please go to the corner of the room and stand with your back to the door. There will be no further warnings given.'

'Please,' Emily said, 'just do as they say.' Her mind had fixated on the possibility of being free once the experiment was over. At this point, she didn't care what it was just that - the sooner they got on with it, the sooner they could go home.

With no other plan coming to mind, James made his way to the corner and begrudgingly stood with his back to the door. As soon as he was in position the door opened. Neither Emily nor James could see who was coming in, but they could hear them; light feet walking upon the hard floor and the squeak of wheels turning on an old trolley as it was pushed into a room. It took everything not to turn around to see what was happening.

A female voice, maybe a nurse, spoke with a soft Welsh accent as she approached Emily first, 'Please stand still as I put this sleeve on your arm.'

'What is it?'

'It's to take your blood pressure,' the woman said, speaking in a kind tone which neither of the "prisoners" had been expecting to hear. 'Nothing to worry about.'

'Okay.'

The nurse strapped the sleeve around Emily's skinny bicep. Once it was velcro-ed into position, she said, 'You're going to feel it tighten around your arm.' With that, she turned the machine on. The band around Emily's arm inflated, squeezing her bicep in the process. It stopped when the machine gave an audible beep and then slowly deflated. A few more seconds and the nurse said, 'All done.' She removed the sleeve and carefully hung it on a small hook on the side of the blood pressure machine's metal stand. She picked up a thermometer box, which came with a small probe attached via a wire, and handed the probe to Emily. 'If you can please place that under your tongue so I can take your temperature.' Emily did as she was told, closing her mouth around it in the process. She stood awkwardly for a few seconds before the nurse said, 'Okay that's fine, thank you.' Emily removed the probe and handed it back.

The nurse replaced the plastic cover on the end of the probe to ensure James had a fresh one before she wheeled the trolley over to his side of the room. She repeated the process with him following the given instructions with minimal interaction. Once she was done, she put a menu on each of their beds before she left the room. The overhead light clicked as it turned from red back to white.

'Is that it?' James slowly turned around first, followed closely by Emily. Given how empty the room was, their eyes were immediately drawn to the menus left on their beds. 'Are you even hungry?'

Emily said, 'Not really.' Food was the last thing on their minds given their predicament. It also didn't help that there was very much a "hospital" feel to the room, and, in their minds, they pictured the choices being made up of plastic food, quickly reheated ahead of being served. Regardless, they each took their menu and scanned the offerings; both were suitably impressed. 'Okay, not quite what I was expecting.' She noticed the menu had lobster as a choice. Even if she were starving, she couldn't envision herself sitting down to eat a lobster dinner all the while she was stressing about her daughter's whereabouts.

It wasn't even her whereabouts that was stressing her either. Even if she was at home, safe and sound, she knew her little girl would still be worried about where her mum was. Perhaps, she thought, it would help if they'd let her at least call home to say she was "safe" and that, hopefully, she would be home soon? It wouldn't hurt to ask at the next given opportunity, she thought. Emily walked back over to the mirror and gently knocked on it in an effort to gain their attention, should they have been looking elsewhere. 'I was wondering if it was possible to call home and let my daughter know I am okay? I know she will be worried about me.' Her request was met with silence. ' Desperate to get the call, she promised, 'I won't tell her where I am.' A silly thing to say really, given she *couldn't* tell her anything. 'I won't mention the experiment. I'll just say that I've had to go away on business for a while and that I'll see her soon.' Still nothing.

James said, 'I doubt they'll let you call home.'

'They might.' She tried calling through again, 'One of your staff can stand by the phone. If I go to say anything you don't like, you can just hang up the call. Or I could pre-record an audio message that you can send her? Please. She'll be worried about me.'

James tossed the menu to one side. They'd already said they'd chosen the meals for the rest of the day and, even if he was hungry now, he had no idea what he'd be in the mood for tomorrow. 'How long do you think they'll keep us in here for?'

Emily couldn't answer him. 'I don't know.' All she could think was, 'Hopefully not long.'

Chapter Eight

There was no clock in the room and neither James nor Emily were wearing a watch. They had been before the experiment had started but, along with the rest of their clothes, their watches had also been removed and taken away. All they could do was guess the time and, with how they tired they were now, all they could presume was, that it was late.

The nurse had come in one more time to take their vitals. On her second visit, she brought them some cheese and cucumber sandwiches and a cup of tea. For the drink, the milk and sugar were kept separately in a little carton and a small packet - just in case they wanted their tea without either option.

Emily also asked the nurse if she could make a call but was told such a request wasn't within the nurse's capabilities. She did, at least, say she would pass the request on although, after she'd left, James had warned Emily not to get her hopes up.

Other than that, there was nothing else of note. James had given Emily a little about his background, that he worked alone and where he worked; the last thing he could recall, before finding himself in the room, was being at the office. Emily had said she'd been running errands for the day and was on her way to pick her daughter up from school. She also had no recollection beyond being in the car.

At one point James had even suggested a game of I-Spy to help pass the time but there wasn't much in the room to make a game of it and, as such, it was pretty short-lived.

Tired, they'd both gone to their beds. The room was warm due to the overbearing light and lack of ventilation and windows so there were no blankets with which to cover themselves.

Both had used the pillows to try and shield their eyes from the room's brightness but, with no other pillow to rest their head on, it wasn't exactly comfortable for either of them and they both tossed and turned.

James was the first to sit up, tossing the pillow across the room towards the mirror out of frustration. He glanced over to Emily hoping she'd do the same, so he'd at least have someone to talk to. She didn't. All she did was pull the pillow tighter over her head, as though trying to shield herself from both the light *and* the noise he was making. James took the hint and tried to keep it down, if only to be considerate to his new room-mate. He quietly sighed; a thought in his head that maybe this would have been easier had he known *why* they were there.

His eyes drifted to the mirror. He tried to imagine who was on the other side. Was there someone still watching them even though they were trying to rest? Or was the room beyond empty now; the workers having long since left and retired to their own homes. Their own comfortable beds for a restful night's sleep ahead of starting their shift in the morning? He couldn't imagine them just stepping away. *Someone* would be there watching if only to stop any potential problems; skeleton staff who'd be able to raise an alarm. Tired, and grumpy, he couldn't help himself; he raised his middle finger and held it up high for whoever would be able to see it. He mouthed, *Fuck you.*

Under her pillow, hidden from both those watching through the mirror and James, Emily was unable to sleep. Her mind was stuck on looped thoughts of her daughter, playing over and over. The thoughts made her feel sick as they twisted her gut and knotted up her intestines. While she didn't want to ever forget her daughter, and never would, she would have given anything to have a break from the thoughts, if only for a moment; long enough to drift off to sleep.

With such raw thoughts, Emily was barely able to stop herself from openly weeping. If she was at home, or at the very least in a private room, she wouldn't have cared and would have let the tears flow. Here though, with an audience, she was desperate to keep them in. Even so, a stray tear rolled down her cheek. Buried beneath the pillow, she was oblivious to the fact that the tear was white.

* * * * *

BEFORE

Emily slammed her fist on the car's horn, not that it would make a difference. It was satisfying though, and it also triggered a chain reaction of other frustrated drivers doing the same.

There was an unannounced road closure up ahead which was causing mayhem to the school traffic. What made it worse was that she was already running late after getting caught up in the supermarket. There'd been an elderly woman in the queue before her, and it was only after the cashier had scanned all her items that she realised she'd mistakenly left her purse at home. First there was embarrassment, then there were tears - none of which was helped by the clueless attendant working the till.

Emily had blamed herself. The self-service desks were empty, but she hated using them so joined the queue for the manned station. Had she just used the self-serve, she'd have been in and out with plenty of time to spare. In the end a suited and booted office worker stepped in and paid the woman's bill for her, much to her relief and gratitude. Emily thought that would have been the end of it but, no. There'd *then* been a five minute back and forth where the old woman was *insisting* on taking the man's details so she could get the money back to him. Meanwhile *he* was insisting that it was "on him" and payback wouldn't have been necessary. It was, he'd said, his good deed for the day; one which got Emily thinking whether she should try pretending she'd left her purse at home too. Maybe she would have given it a try, if she hadn't already been concerned about the time.

The traffic inched forward as the temporary lights changed long enough to let two cars pass through. Emily was now one car length away from another turn-off. She wasn't as familiar with the other route but knew it would, eventually, get her to - she hoped - a clearer route; one on which she could make up some time. There was fifteen minutes of the car journey left and only five minutes until the school kicked out.

Another car horn sounded off from somewhere behind where Emily was stuck. She looked in her rear-view mirror, amused that she'd started this off. Perhaps, she hoped, the workers would set a more realistic timer on the traffic lights to give the traffic more chance to get anywhere.

Up ahead the lights changed from red to green. Again, a couple of cars managed to get through before it changed back again but - it wasn't a problem for Emily this time. It had made enough space for her to reach the turning she'd been eyeing up. With a flick of her finger, she indicated to the left and turned down the narrow road, grateful to be moving again - even if she didn't know the exact way from here.

'All roads lead to Rome,' she muttered.

* * * * *

Emily's thoughts were disturbed by the *click* of the light: White turned to red.

James called out, 'You awake?'

From under the pillow, Emily said, 'Yes.'

She put the pillow to the side and sat up, giving James the chance to see her face for the first time since they'd tried burying themselves, hiding from the light. 'What's that?'

Emily frowned. 'What's what?'

'On your face.'

Emily wiped what she thought had been a tear. She looked down and saw the white liquid. 'What *is* that?'

The voice came over the speaker, 'Please move to the corner.'

Chapter Nine

'Do you know what this is?' Emily held her hand out in front of her so the nurse, standing behind with her monitoring equipment, could see the white smear mark.

The nurse had already taken Emily's vitals, and everything seemed normal and while the white appearance of the tears may have been somewhat alarming, it was "normal". 'I wouldn't worry,' she said, 'it's just a side effect of the medication.'

Emily frowned. 'But I haven't had any med…' Her voice trailed off when she realised that was how they'd got her into the room. They had injected her with God only knew what so as to knock her out long enough to get her into the room.

'So, can we expect white urine and white shit when we go to the bathroom? Because, I'm just saying, that's kind of a good thing to know *before* it happens and freaks us out,' James said from his corner.

The nurse pushed the trolley over to James. Because they'd been through the process more than once now, she didn't feel the need to give a running commentary as to what she was doing. She just got on with it while James "willingly" stood there.

He continued, 'Is there anything else we need to know about this *medication*?'

'Side effects are rare,' the nurse said in a very matter-of-fact tone, 'you have nothing to worry about.'

'Really?' James couldn't help but laugh. There was nothing to worry about? They'd woken in a room they didn't know. They were a part of an experiment they never signed up for. Now they'd just learned they'd been given medication they never consented to which was toxic enough to change the colour of Emily's tears. What else were they going to find?

After the nurse took James's temperature, he continued, 'If there's nothing to worry about, there'd be no need for all the secrecy.'

The nurse made a note of all the statistics she'd recorded and started to clear away her equipment. She explained, 'I'm sorry but that's nothing to do with me. I'm just here to take your vitals.'

'So, you can't tell us anything?'

'I'm not allowed.'

'Not allowed?'

'No.'

'Says who?' James was hoping she'd slip up and give *something* away. He already knew it wouldn't be enough to fill in all the missing blanks but, slowly, he might be able to start piecing the puzzle together.

Before James scared the woman out of the room, Emily jumped in with a question of her own, 'Can you ask the people in charge if I can *please* call home?'

'I'll pass the message on,' the nurse said.

She didn't sound as sincere as Emily had hoped so she continued, 'I tried calling through the mirror, but no one answered. I said, I can even pre-record a message... So they know I am not going to say anything that would upset them. I just want her to know that I'm okay, so she doesn't worry.'

'Of course. I understand.'

One final push, Emily said, 'And if they're agreeable... It means I can relax more for the experiment.' A little blackmail, she figured. If they help her out, she'd be more keen to help them out with whatever they wanted.

'I will let them know,' the nurse said. Before they could ask any more questions, or make any further demands, she pushed her trolley towards the closed door. When she was close enough, it opened from the other side. She stepped out. 'We've gone to the trouble of choosing breakfast for you,' she said. 'If you want your own choice for the other meals today, please do let us know your preferences within the next few minutes.'

James called over his shoulder, 'How do we know what the next few minutes are when we don't have a clock in here?'

The nurse smiled. She knew what he was trying to do. Instead of answering, she gave a nod, and an unseen person closed the door on her behalf. The light switched to white, freeing Emily and James from the corners of the room.

'They're not going to let you make a call. They're not going to let you record a message. You need to stop with that and think more about how we get out of here,' James said. There was a level of aggression in his voice which made Emily feel uncomfortable. She didn't bother trying to argue back with him, pointing out it was easy for him to say given he didn't have anyone waiting at home for him. If he had a child, he'd understand. That being said, she also knew they couldn't exactly make plans to escape - not while they were being watched.

If only to get away from a potentially uncomfortable conversation, Emily picked her menu up again. She scanned the list, despite still not feeling hungry. 'She said they've already chosen breakfast for us. I guess we know what the time is at least.'

James grunted. Clearly he was one of those who struggled with his moods when he didn't get enough sleep. Emily couldn't blame him. She was feeling the stress of the situation - and lack of sleep - too. He walked over to his bed and picked the menu up. A quick scan and he shouted to the mirror, 'I'll have the steak. Medium. Crumble for dessert. Ham sandwich later but - I don't want the mustard.'

A voice came through immediately, 'Your order has been accepted.'

Emily shrugged. 'I'll have the salad.' It was the lightest thing on the menu. 'Just some toast later.'

The voice asked, 'Dessert?'

'No thank you,' Emily said. She'd never really had a sweet tooth, unlike her daughter who needed to be convinced to eat the main meal first. She had a nasty habit of just picking at it so as to save room for pudding.

'Your order has been accepted.'

Emily resisted the urge to ask about the call again.

The voice spoke, 'Breakfast will be delivered in an hour. For making it through your first night successfully, and without problems, we will now turn the light off until breakfast is ready. Goodnight.'

The light switched off, plunging the room into a blissful blackness. Both James and Emily didn't waste any time in trying to catch a quick little nap in the welcome darkness.

Part Three
Before

Chapter Ten

Dr. Chappo stalked through the long corridors with purpose; a concerned look on his face after a troubling call from the control room had disturbed an autopsy he was performing.

His colleague, Dr. Schwartz, was standing at the far end of the next corridor he turned down. She was waiting for him with a similar expression on his face. 'Please,' she said, 'take your time.' Her voice was laced with sarcasm.

'I'm here, aren't I? You didn't have to wait for me.'

'And if they turn violent?'

Dr. Chappo laughed. 'You're expecting me to save you?' When he reached her, they continued down the next corridor in perfect step with one another. There was an armed security guard at the far end, waiting by a closed door. Dr. Chappo called out, 'We're the first here?'

The guard nodded. 'Yes, sir.'

'Open the door.'

By the time the guard opened the door, both Dr. Chappo and Dr. Schwartz were able to stride right into the room; white walls, white floor, a single bed bolted to the floor along one of the walls, a toilet and a two-way mirror on the wall opposite. A naked woman was having a seizure on the bed; her eyes rolling to the back of her head as a white froth coughed from her mouth as she choked on it.

Dr. Schwartz grabbed the pillow and moved it, positioning it in such a way so as to block the fitting woman from hitting her head against the wall. 'Do we know how long she's been fitting for?'

Dr. Chappo shrugged. 'Does it matter? Look at her. She's fucked. He took a step back and leaned out of the open doorway. With a nod of his head, he gestured for the guard to do the right thing.

The guard understood the assignment; he stepped into the room and pulled a pistol from his holster. Without so much of a warning to the oblivious Dr. Schwartz, the guard put the gun to the woman's head and pulled the trigger. The woman stopped fitting instantly as her black brains covered both the wall and the pillow.

Dr. Schwartz jumped back, shocked. 'Are you *insane*?'

Her words weren't aimed to the guard who was busy re-holstering his weapon. They were aimed at Dr. Chappo. He pointed to the black splatter as it dribbled down the wall. 'I told you. She's fucked. The rot's already set in. Only way to learn from them when they get to this stage is through opening them up, not comforting them when they have a seizure.'

Dr. Schwartz reached into the inner pocket of her white lab coat and pulled out a handkerchief. Worried some of the "rot" had hit her in the face, she used the handkerchief to mop herself clean. 'I could have got it in my mouth.'

'And if you had, all that would have happened was you'd get a grotesque aftertaste. It's nothing to worry about.' Dr. Chappo laughed. 'You're new here but you'll get used to how things run around here but, get this in your head sooner rather than later, these are not people. They are our experiments and, as all good scientists know, you need to know when an experiment is over.' He gestured towards the body. 'And this one is over.'

Dr. Schwartz tossed the handkerchief on the floor. 'I didn't sign up for this.'

'But you did though.' He looked at the body. 'We're done here anyway. See to it she's brought down to the morgue, and I'll open her up properly once I'm done with the current lump of meat on my table.' He didn't wait for her to argue with him and promptly left the room, keen to get back to his work. If she had a problem, she could take it Dr. Kiefel and have it out with her. And if she did? He didn't care. Had it been Dr. Kiefel in the room with them now, it would have had exactly the same ending. The only difference was it would have been Kiefel who'd have given the order to pull the trigger.

Dr. Schwartz turned her attention to the guard who'd repositioned himself by the door. He was staring at the mirror. She knew he wasn't looking at his own reflection. She turned to the mirror and asked, 'What are you looking at?' Knowing there'd be no answer, she stormed from the room. *That mess* was someone else's problem to deal with.

On the other side of the mirror, Dr. Mary Kiefel had been watching everything. Dr. Chappo was right; she wouldn't have handled the situation any differently although she did have *some* concerns: Why in the hell had the new doctor tried to *help* a lost cause? She thought the given training had been pretty clear about how things operated here but clearly not. She sighed; it was nothing that wasn't trainable.

A phone rung from a table across the other side of the room, next to an intercom system. A sitting guard answered it. '414. Yes, she's here. Hold on.' He swivelled in his chair and held the phone towards Kiefel. 'It's for you.'

Kiefel took the phone from the guard. 'This is Dr. Kiefel.'

'Yeah it's me.' Dr. Chappo was calling from the morgue. 'You're going to need to come and see this,' he said. Kiefel could tell from his voice it wasn't good news. 'I'm back in the morgue.'

She said nothing. She handed the phone back to the guard and left the room. The guard stayed at his post; he knew it wouldn't be long before another guest was moved into the room. *It was never very long.*

Chapter Eleven

The compound was on the edge of town, a couple of miles from the financial district where most of the large corporations had their head offices. Backing onto the start of the English countryside, the impressive complex was set back behind a large security fence built to keep trespassers from breaking in. With a long, gated driveway, lined with tall oak trees, it was nigh on impossible to see the actual building from the roadside. Before the gates were opened, all potential visitors were required to stop by the security office to show their I.D. Those with appointments were given instructions on how to get to the main reception area while those who were just chancing their luck were turned away.

The complex was a modern design with a glass fronted building through which visitors could see large open office spaces with people working behind their desks. It was a twenty-four hour operation although, at night, it was mostly manned by a skeleton crew. Behind the thick walls of the open offices, there was a network of corridors. For the most part, these weren't as stark as the white rooms in which the experiments were conducted. There was modern art hanging on the walls, tall potted plants in the corners and the occasional coffee machine where employees could get their hot drinks.

Push beyond the main part of the building, going deeper towards where the experiments were, and the corridors started to become more austere; a money-saving exercise, not that money was a great concern to the company, as not many people had access to these parts; each corridor hidden behind a locked door which required a keycard with high clearance levels to access.

Kiefel's card got her to all parts of the building. To get from one corridor to the next, she tapped it against a metal box on the door.

A red light on said box would turn green once the door was ready to be opened.

She walked into the morgue where Dr. Chappo was filming the corpse he'd been working on before being called to where the woman was having the seizure. 'What's the issue?' Dr. Chappo stepped to the side so she could see for herself. She stopped in her tracks. 'What the hell is that?'

The naked body on the table had been cut open from neck to abdomen; not just the skin but the rib cage too, giving Dr. Chappo full access to the black organs within. In the centre of the body there was a large black, pulsating mass. A stick thin arm, no more than thirty centimetres in length and with a clawed hand - the size of an infant's - was reaching out from the tumour-looking lump.

All Dr. Chappo could say was, 'I have no idea. It wasn't there when I went to see the other patient. Came back and this damn thing was reaching out.'

'It looks like it continues up into the neck,' Kiefel said, pointing out how the black mass seemed to have a "spine".

'That's what I thought too but figured I'd be better off calling you first. Want me to open the face?'

Kiefel took the camera from him and kept it pointing towards the body. 'Do it.'

Dr. Chappo picked the bone-saw up from a nearby table and started sawing just beneath the corpse's chin; the noise it made not too dissimilar to a normal saw biting into a thick piece of wood. With the power of the saw and the sharpness of its teeth, it didn't take long to saw through the mouth, through the centre of the nose, between the pure white eyes, into the forehead and through the middle of the cranium. Once he was sure he'd cut enough, he set the blade to one side before choosing a clamp. He slid its closed "mouth" into the gap before, with effort, opening it up and stretching the skull open in the process. He jumped back at the sight of another small black mass nestled within the white. Unlike the one in the stomach, this one had a pair of beady eyes protruding from the top of it. 'The fuck?'

Kiefel caught it all on camera. Watching through the camera's viewfinder, she wasn't sure *what* she was seeing. She lowered the camera and looked with her own eyes. 'Whatever batch this came from, I want it all destroyed,' she said.

'Look,' Dr. Chappo pointed to the mass in the centre of the stomach. Slowly but surely, it was stretching down towards the gut as *it* continued to grow.

Kiefel had seen enough. Whatever this was, it wasn't good. 'Incinerate it,' she ordered.

'You don't want to see what happens?'

'No.' Whatever was happening was not a part of their plan and, as far as she could see, no good could come from it. 'I want you to incinerate it,' she said again. 'Along with any of the batch we have left. Burn it all.'

'While I know another batch is ready for testing, I'm pretty sure they'd already used the same batch this is from for the next experiment. Want to pull the plug on that before it gets started?'

'I think that would be a smart move. No sense wasting time when Sam's breathing down our necks pushing for results.'

Samantha Schlecht was the head of the corporation and was bank-rolling the entire business. While much of the business came from sponsors, and those looking to utilise what they were working on, she also used her own savings to keep things moving along. No one knew exactly where her wealth came from, and no one dared to ask. She was a formidable woman who took no bullshit from anyone and, as such, any conversation with her tended to be one way: Answering her questions and giving her progress updates. It was *very* rare that she'd stop to ask how people were doing on a personal level, and she didn't ever come out on the few work-dos the business organised each year as a "bonus" for the workers. If she felt like someone wasn't yielding the results she wanted, or wasn't pulling their weight, she didn't hesitate to dismiss them - but not after ensuring they signed another non-disclosure agreement; something they also signed before being actively employed there.

While Dr. Chappo didn't usually talk back to Kiefel, once she'd given direction, he couldn't help but wonder what would happen if they did leave this thing to grow? Would it be nothing more than a *monster* writhing around in the remains of those it grew from, or would it eventually break free becoming its own "thing"? If the latter than, perhaps there'd be a use for it in the marketplace. 'While I'm happy to incinerate it, of course…' He hesitated, unsure whether he was about to overstep the mark.

'What is it?'

'I was just wondering whether we should let this grow out and see what happens? We could seal it in one of the rooms and keep watch… If it continues growing and something does end up coming out of it… Surely there'd be a market for that?'

'I think it would scare the shit out of those who'd just lost a loved one,' Kiefel said. 'The last thing they'd want, when dealing with grief, is to see their partner's body birth a monstrosity.'

'Agreed but I wasn't thinking about having them out in the *normal* market. What about if they were given to the military?'

Kiefel could see where Dr. Chappo's brain was leading him. If these people were killed on the front line, it *could* potentially be useful to have something else grow from within their corpses; especially if it had the same memories and thoughts as those they'd grown from. There'd be nothing to stop them from picking up from where the first person dropped and, at the very least, it would be a hell of a distraction to the enemy. She nodded. 'Okay. Put it in one of the spare rooms, seal it in there and we'll put a skeleton crew on it to keep watch.' She continued, 'I watched the new doctor today, with the woman having the seizure… If we do this I want it made very clear that there's *no* helping whatever comes out. If there's a problem, the instructions should be very clear: We go in and we terminate it.'

Dr. Chappo nodded in agreement. 'And the one we're about to start experimenting on now? Do we leave that as planned and see what happens or do we still pull the plug?'

'We can watch it for now,' she said. 'Same again though, the first sign there's a problem…'

'Terminate. Got it.' He added, 'So just so we're singing from the same song sheet, we're leaving that batch alone at the moment?'

'For now.'

Chapter Twelve

It was only two hours into a twelve hour shift and already it had been a hell of a day. When Kiefel stepped into her office and saw Sam Schlecht sitting at her desk, she knew it wasn't about to be getting any better either.

Sam was sitting on Kiefel's side of the desk as though it were her own office. There were a number of open files sprawled across the table in front of her from where she'd spent the last hour going through the various written reports. When Kiefel walked into the room, she didn't even bother to look up before she said, 'Take a seat.'

After the events in The White Room that morning, Kiefel had suspected she'd be seeing Sam today but not like this. She'd presumed she would be getting summoned to her office, which is how it usually worked out if Sam wanted to see her. Feeling somewhat ambushed, Kiefel took a seat. Even so, she tried to keep it polite and as friendly as she dared to get with Sam, 'Good morning.'

'What happened?'

Kiefel didn't need to know what Sam was asking about. Whenever an experiment was terminated, Sam would always be there to ask about it. 'The patient had a seizure,' Kiefel said.

'I saw the footage. Do we know why yet?'

'Dr. Chappo will be performing an autopsy later.'

'Later?' One thing Sam hated was when things such as this were put off until "later". She wanted to know if it was a problem with the serum or whether there were underlying illnesses playing a part in the seizure. "Later" didn't get her the immediate answers she demanded.

'He's just finishing another one off,' Kiefel said. While she didn't like hiding things from Sam, she didn't want to go into the specifics of what she'd just seen with Dr. Chappo. Bringing up the mass would only get more questions asked; questions she wouldn't be able to answer.

'Well tell him I want answers before the end of the day.'

'Of course.'

'The next experiment is ready to start, I trust?'

'Yes.'

'That's good.' Sam leaned back in Kiefel's expensive leather chair. She sighed. 'I honestly thought we would be further along now. I can't pretend I'm not disappointed.'

Kiefel tried to reassure her, 'We're working around the clock.'

'And yet you're not making progress.' She paused a moment before stating, 'Perhaps I need to shake the team up a bit?'

Kiefel knew her job was hanging by a thread. 'I know it doesn't feel like progress is coming as fast as you'd like, and I understand the urgency to get results. I can assure you though that, with each subject used, we're making *some* progress.'

'Hmmmm.' Sam continued, 'I also saw the new doctor and how they responded to the seizure. She is aware this isn't a normal hospital, isn't she?'

'All training has been given,' Kiefel said, 'but I've already made a mental note to pull her to one side to explain things again.'

'Perhaps dumb it down if she is struggling to understand what we are doing here. Or, perhaps, maybe replace her with someone who *does* get it.'

'Dr. Schwartz is very qualified in her field,' Kiefel said. With everything going on at the moment, she didn't want to take time out to interview more candidates. If she could have a word with Dr. Schwartz and make her follow the rules as per her agreement, she knew she had the potential to be an asset to the team.

Unfortunately, Sam didn't see everything these people had to offer; she just seemed to notice when mistakes were made. 'I'm sure that once I have a word with her, she'll be a credit to the company.'

'I'm glad you seem so sure of her but, okay. Make sure you talk to her today. If we have another repeat performance of this morning, I would sooner cut our loses and look to employ someone else.'

'I understand.'

'I also think we could expand the experiments. With that in mind, I've ordered more beds. They should be here tomorrow morning. Once they get here, I want all hands on deck to get them installed so we can run multiple experiments at once.' Sam continued, 'Like I said, "I want to start seeing more progress.'

The thought of running multiple experiments at once didn't fill Kiefel with much joy given the work that went into monitoring just one at a time, but she kept her opinion to herself. If Sam wanted something done, it would be done. There'd be no "ands" or "buts".

'And just in case your new worker doesn't take your words onboard, I think it would be prudent to run another recruitment drive. It wouldn't hurt to have more hands on deck anyway.' The first thing Sam had said which made Kiefel slightly happier, not that she enjoyed the interview process. If they were to be running more than one test at a time, it would definitely make their lives easier to have extra hands on deck. 'Well then,' Sam concluded, 'I think that pretty much sums everything up that I had to say. Tell Dr. Chappo to report to me as soon as he opens up today's patient and, other than that, I'll touch base with you tomorrow.'

'Okay.'

As Sam stood, so too did Kiefel. She watched as her boss had another quick glance around the room. Without further words, she left, closing the door behind her. Kiefel walked round to her chair and slumped down. *A hell of a day.*

Chapter Thirteen

Dr. Chappo wheeled the corpse towards the white room where the last experiment had been terminated. The room hadn't been cleaned; the woman's blackened brains still dribbled down the wall. Normally, before new experiments were brought in, the rooms would have a deep clean but given the state of *this* experiment - cleanliness wasn't a necessity. It could wait until however this one ended.

In life, the dead person had been Ariel Kollmansberger; someone's daughter, someone's partner. When she had been brought to the compound, all trace of identity had been stripped away from her and she was left with nothing more than a number; not that she ever knew what the number was. Just as others had begged for freedom, demanded answers and begrudgingly followed the given instructions, fearful of the ever present threat of punishment, she died with none of what she sought. One minute she had been eating her breakfast, the next she was sweating profusely before dropping her cereal bowl to the floor ahead of a seizure so violent she had bitten her tongue off and dislocated her neck. As black blood poured from her mouth, the door opened - no changing of the room's light for this visit - and a guard came in with fresh instructions radioed through. He put the gun to her head and pulled the trigger. A clean shot between her eyes and the floor was painted in the same black ooze that had vomited from her mouth.

As Dr. Chappo approached the door, the waiting guard warned, 'This room isn't ready yet.'

'It's clean enough for this,' Dr. Chappo said. 'Open the door.'

The guard did as he was instructed.

Although the guards had also signed non-disclosure agreements when they had accepted the role within the corporation, Dr. Chappo had purposefully covered Ariel's corpse with a black sheet to hide what was happening within the deceased woman's insides; a sight sure enough to make even the most hardened of souls panic or, at the very least, *talk*.

He pushed the trolley into the room as the guard asked, 'Did you need a hand with it?'

'No. Please wait outside.' The other body had already been removed, although the putrid puddle of leaking brains and broken skull fragments remained. Dr. Chappo stopped the trolley by the bed and turned to face the guard. He was watching from the door. 'If you can please close the door. When I am ready, I'll knock.'

The guard nodded. He stepped back and closed the door, leaving Dr. Chappo alone.

Chappo wasted no time. He lifted the sheet and recoiled in horror at the sight of the mass writhing around within Ariel's body. In the short walk from mortuary to room, it had almost doubled in size; its hand now the size of a young child and clear signs of a brain forming within the cut-open cranium. Grabbed Ariel's body by its feet, he pulled it from trolley to bed without giving much thought, or concern, to potentially hurting the *thing* within.

Once it was on the bed, he took a step back and watched as the hand continued stretching from within while trying to grab a hold of something. What it was looking for exactly, Chappo had no idea. Curious, and with a gloved hand, he cautiously reached towards the hand. Their fingertips barely touched when Chappo had a change of heart and abruptly pulled away. Without knowing what this thing was, there was no way of being sure what it would do if they were to "shake" hands. There was also no way of knowing as to whether it was toxic.

Dr. Chappo flung the sheet back onto the trolley and wheeled it over towards the door. He stopped in his tracks when, from within the body, he heard the words, ‘Mummy…?’ Slowly, unsure whether he’d really heard anything at all, he turned back to the body. Slower still, he made his way back over to the bed whereupon he peered into the cracked skull. The black mass within, with its beady little eyes, was staring right at him. Just beneath the eyes, a mouth had formed. ‘Mummy?’

Dr. Chappo stumbled back in horror as another hand reached from within, stretching out towards where he was standing. In that moment he regretted his curiosity in seeing how this played out and wished he could have just turned back the clock and agreed to incinerating whatever the fuck this was.

‘Mummy…’

Chapter Fourteen

On the other side of the complex, Dr. Sophie Hall and Dr. Java Henderson were watching their own experiments interact through the two-way mirror. Sophia and Mark Flemmich, a rare case in which the two people put into the room together actually knew one another.

Hall and Henderson were more excited about running this experiment because, not only were they using a new serum batch, they were also going to be able to skip past the usual way these tests started; the subjects being deeply suspicious of one another and potentially ruining the experiment before it had a chance to start. At least, here, they wouldn't be sitting in silence and nor would they be trying to kill one another. Instead, Hall and Henderson hoped there would be a level of calm they'd not seen before while the subjects simply did as they were told.

Mark had woken up first. He'd run over to Sophia and shaken her from her slumber, keen to ensure she was okay and relieved when she did open her eyes. 'What? What is it?' Her eyes focused and the confusion from being woken so abruptly turned to one of sheer panic. 'Where are we?'

Dr. Hall sat down in one of the chairs. She reached for a file and started making notes; the first entry of many which showcased they were "okay" upon waking. The first experiments hadn't got much past this initial box-tick after the test subjects woke-up while being violently sick and bleeding black blood from nostrils, mouth, ears and tear ducts. The seizures were quick to follow. She asked Henderson, 'What's your thoughts then? How far are these two getting?'

Henderson peered over Hall's shoulder and down at the file on the desk. There was an A4 sheet of boxes to tick and, to date, they'd only ever made it to the halfway mark. 'I think these could go the distance.' A belief held due to the fact that it was husband and wife together; a supportive couple to help ease some of the stress. Henderson had always said putting two strangers in the room, and in this environment, only made the stress worse which, in turn, sped up the time in which the seizures came. She'd voiced this to Kiefel, but her words had fallen on deaf ears.

'I reckon they'll do worse,' Hall said.

'Worse?'

'A married couple locked in a room together? If they're anything like my mum and dad…'

'Hmmm. Didn't think of that.' She pushed the file away and turned towards the mirror.

Mark had his head pressed up against it. He tapped on the window. 'Hello? Anyone in there?'

Sophia was pushing the handless door to no avail. They *always* tried the door. Did any of them ever think it would actually open?

Hall asked, 'Did you want to do the honours and speak to them?'

Henderson declined the invitation, 'No. I don't like talking on the intercom. It's off-putting hearing the sound of my own voice.'

Hall sighed. She hated it too and yet it was always her who seemed to get roped into speaking to the subjects whenever she was on duty. She wheeled herself across to the other side of the room where the microphone for the intercom system was set up. Keen to get this part over with, she reached for the on-switch. She stopped as an alarm rang through the non-sound-proofed rooms of the complex signalling a problem in one of the other rooms.

There was a panel on the wall opposite the mirror showcasing different room numbers with lights beneath the numbers themselves. Room 4 was flashing.

Henderson frowned. 'I thought that room was empty? Didn't the patient literally have a seizure less than an hour ago?'

'Maybe a mistake?' Mistake or not, it didn't matter. They knew the rules. When the internal alarm ran in the back rooms, they knew they had to investigate. Dr. Hall got up first and made her way from the room. Dr. Henderson followed albeit begrudgingly. Never once had she done anything but watch when one of the alarms went off. It was always the senior doctors who rushed to get involved where applicable but, nine times out of ten, it was a quick "problem" often resumed with nothing more than a single bullet to the temple.

They hurried down the corridor and turned into the next. A guard ran towards them, not to lead them to where they needed to be but, because he was running away from the situation; panic in his eyes as he muttered something inaudible.

'Well, that can't be good,' Hall said.

Both doctors stopped in their tracks as an oily, black humanoid shape staggered through Room 4's open door. In its claw-like hand, it held Dr. Chappo's severed head by a tuft of its hair. It turned, yellow beady eyes, and locked its gaze to the two approaching doctors.

Hall found no words.

Henderson stuttered, 'Wh… what the fuck is that?'

For a moment they are just stood and stared at one another before the creature said, 'Mummy?'

A gun-shot rang through the air, startling both women, as another guard came round the corner and - without stopping to think - opened fire. The first shot hit the creature as a second and third shot were fired in quick succession. Both bullets hit the intended target. The bullets passed straight through it's moist body, digging into the wall behind. The creature didn't react to any of the shots. It just stood there, watching. Waiting.

'Mummy?'

'Get behind me,' the guard warned the women. They didn't need telling twice and backed up. The guard stepped forward and emptied the clip. The bullet between the eyes was the one which dropped the creature. As it fell, it released its grip of Chappo's head which also hit the floor with a heavy thud. Another accident at work; another payout to a family waiting at home.

Part Four
Today

Chapter Fifteen

The nurse's name was Tammie Baade. While she didn't enjoy the job, the money kept her going back for her twelve hour shifts. For the most part it was easy enough; she'd go into the room, she's take the subject's temperature, she would check their blood pressure, leave them a menu and leave. If the subjects tried to engage in conversation, depending on her mood, she would either have a brief, non-personal conversation or she'd keep things professional and only discuss what she was needing to do. On the many times they tried asking her what was happening, where they were or when they could leave - she'd never give a straight answer and would, instead, say it would be a conversation for the doctors.

Emily had made the same request every day. She wanted to call home and let her daughter know she was okay or, at the very least, leave a voice message for her to stop her from worrying. Tammie knew the answer would be "no" but she also knew, if she said as such, it would cause potential problems. Telling Emily that she'd pass her message on to the doctors bought her time and saved immediate conflict.

Tammie was in charge of overseeing James and Emily. They'd been in their room for a little under a month now despite their calls to be released and their darkening moods; depression deepening with each passing day.

The part of the job Tammie hated was when she needed to draw blood. For a nurse in a normal hospital, this wasn't a problem. The worst they had to contend with was hard-to-find-veins and the occasional patient passing out. Here though, she not only had to take blood of someone who was unwilling, but she also had to try and downplay the colouring of the blood once it was drawn.

Why does it look black?

It's just the way the light is hitting it.

And, more recently:

Why does it look white?

The white was almost impossible to explain. It couldn't be passed off as a trick of the light. All Tammie could say was, 'It's perfectly normal, just a side effect of the medication you were given prior to your arrival.' While it explained the colouring, it didn't give further insight into *what* the subjects had been injected with which caused more questions as they enquired about *that* instead. The answer to that? 'The doctor will explain everything in time.' Again, Tammie knew the explanations wouldn't come. Perhaps, if they made it to the end of the experiment, it would but, so far, none of them had got that far.

Tammie didn't know what fate awaited Emily and James. None of the workers did. The "white blood" was still relatively new and while other subjects hadn't survived for more than a few weeks, they still lasted longer than those who had veins full of *black* and, with each tweak to the meds, that timeframe was getting a little longer each time.

The doctors' plans were first to find a medication which saw the subjects reach the end of the experiment and then to find a way to get the blood colour back to its natural shade. In its present state, the medication couldn't be released to the open market as it would cause too much concern and make it obvious to others that it had been used. Once that final box was ticked, it would be released, and the promised wealth would begin to roll in. Tammie couldn't *wait* for that day, even though it then raised the question as to what happened to her job. Would they keep her on the books, would there be other departments she could move to, or would she find herself back on the unemployment line? *Tomorrow's problem.*

'How's it going in there?' The guard standing at the door to Emily and James's room was always chatty. Tammie's colleagues joked that it was because he'd taken a shine to Tammie, most of the men had, but she dismissed their comments, stating he was just bored. On this side of the building, the corridors were narrow walk-throughs with plain white walls and not much to see or do. At least the guards in the viewing room had a computer to look at, and the two-way mirror allowing them to watch what was happening in the room. Tammie couldn't even begin to imagine how boring the job was for those who worked *this* side of the wall.

'So far so good,' Tammie said as she pulled her trolley down the corridor towards him.

'Reckon this is the one?' There was hope in the guard's voice. The way he saw it, the moment the experiment was over, he'd be moved to a more interesting part of the building to watch over. Standing here with only the occasional person to talk to, the days dragged, and he struggled to remain focused.

Tammie shrugged. 'Who knows?' While she hoped the experiment was nearing an end, she never presumed things were going to be "okay". With each and every test they were getting closer to where they needed to be but the moment someone said, *I think we've cracked it*, something would go wrong, and they'd be back to square one. Now it was better to not even try and jinx it.

'Well, here's hoping,' the guard said.

When Tammie was close enough, the guard shouldered his rifle and pulled the door open. She stepped into the room with a, 'Thank you.'

'Knock when you're ready,' he said as he shut her in.

Chapter Sixteen

The room was illuminated with the red light. James and Emily were standing in their corners. The smell of shit lingered in the air from where one of them had made use of the toilet, almost making Tammie gag as she breathed it in. She didn't pass comment on it as she wheeled her way over to Emily first.

'Did you pass my message on? About making the call home?'

'I did,' Tammie lied.

'And what did they say?'

'I'm sorry but they don't really discuss things like that with me.' Not a lie. Even if she had passed the request on, they wouldn't have discussed it with her; they'd have talked it through with those on the same level as them.

'So far we've done everything that's been asked of us,' James said. 'When all this started we were told of rewards and yet we've had nothing but empty words.'

'I will pass on your concerns,' Tammie said, not wanting to get stuck in a conversation she had no control over.

Yeah, so they can ignore it. You realise this is completely illegal, right? You're keeping us detained against our will, with no idea as to why we're actually here…' It was clear from his tone that he'd had enough; a problem for Tammie as it meant there was potential for him to fight back and, if he did, that would be the end of the experiment, and they'd be forced to start over.

Tammie didn't try and calm his temper. She knew there was no point. Whatever she said to calm the situation would only serve to make it worse. Instead, she turned her attention as to why she was there. 'I'm going to start with the blood pressure, then the temperature.' She added, 'After that, I'll be taking some blood.'

James said, 'No. I don't think so. Temperature, fine. Blood pressure, fine. You're not taking my blood.'

Emily was more obedient but only because she wanted to make that call home to her daughter. She presented her arm. Tammie set about taking her blood pressure before Emily had a chance to change her mind.

'How many other people have you got locked against their will? How many other people are you illegally running experiments on? Do you honestly think we won't go to the authorities when we are finally released?' As he stood in his corner, James's temper continued to rise, as did the volume with which he spoke.

A stern voice came over the intercom, 'Please calm down.'

James snapped straight back, 'No! I won't *calm* down! Tell us what the hell is going on or just let us go! You have no right to keep us here against our will.'

The voice said again, sterner still, '*Calm* down.'

'Fuck you.'

Knowing they were finally being listened to, Emily repeated her earlier request, 'Can I *please* call home and let my daughter know I'm okay? If you let me do that, I don't even care if you let him go and just keep me here. Please. I just want to talk to her.'

Tammie could only see this escalating. She removed the blood-pressure monitor sleeve and took a step back away from Emily; a sideways glance to the mirror. She knew all eyes were on them from the other room. She also knew the probable outcome for how this would end, with the bubbling tempers and overall stress continuing to rise.

'Your third and final warning,' the voice came through, 'please calm down and let our staff complete their tasks.'

James wasn't having it. 'Fuck you, fuck the nurse, fuck the room and *fuck* whatever the hell this is!' He turned from the corner of the room and stormed over to Tammie. She stumbled back, unsure whether he was about to lash out. He was, but not at her. He grabbed the trolley and toppled it over before doing the same to the blood monitor machine. Tammie wasted no time; she hurried over to the door and knocked on it. As it opened, James stormed towards the exit point only to stop in his tracks when the guard appeared with his weapon aimed and ready to use. Tammie beat a hasty retreat, barely containing her tears. 'Put the gun down and face me like a real man,' James hissed.

The guard smiled. All it took was one word through the intercom system and his finger would squeeze the trigger and all aggressiveness would stop. No word came. He slowly backed out of the room before pulling the door shut.

For a moment, James and Emily stood in silence. Eventually, she asked, 'What have you done?' If there ever was a chance to get that call home, she knew she'd lost it now.

'What have I done? I've stood up against these assholes! They have no right to keep us here, no right to keep you from your daughter and yet here we are… And you're playing nice with them. Why? Because you want to see your daughter again? Plot-twist: You will *never* see your daughter again. Do you honestly believe they're going to release us and let us go back to our lives as though none of this happened? Never going to happen. We were dead the moment we got here.'

Emily sat on the edge of her bed where she started to cry, tears of white. She wiped them away as the door opened for a second time. The guard walked in with his gun raised, pointed towards James. He made no effort to protect himself for what came next; he simply closed his eyes and waiting for the bullet thumping into his body, penetrating whatever organ it hit. No shot came. Slowly, he opened his eyes again. The guard had his finger to his ear, pushing an ear-piece, listening to the voice speaking to him.

'You're lucky,' the guard said. He lowered his gun and stepped from the room, closing the door behind him.

James frowned. 'What the fuck was that about?'

Chapter Seventeen

Kiefel had spared James. She'd come into the room and witnessed the whole outburst and the way Dr. Ashley Chmielewski had handled it. The moment Dr. Chmielewski had seen that things were past the point of no return she'd acted decisively, telling the guard to put James down; the perfect way of handling such situations as, if they were going to be trouble, it wasn't worth continuing wasting time with them. Not when they could simply start again. On this occasion though, Kiefel went against protocol. She explained, 'These two have come further than any of the others we've used before. We're better off leaving them in there, delivering their food only and watching how it plays out.'

Chmielewski nodded, showing that she understood the new instructions. 'You want to stop taking their vitals?'

'Out of all the different tests we've run, vitals have always remained consistent. I think it's fair to say we have enough data at this point.' Even on the day of their seizures, none of the other test subjects had ever shown a problem through blood pressure monitoring or their temperatures. They were one hundred percent fine right up until the seizure. Even after cutting them up, the earlier test subjects at least, everything seemed *normal* within too. The black ink-like blood only showing in later subjects; a problem which had been replaced now with white fluid pumping through the veins of the later experiments. She said again, 'Let it run.'

With nothing else to see, Kiefel turned for the door. It opened, revealing Sam to be standing there. 'If you're not too busy, may I have a word?'

Kiefel's heart skipped a beat, but she hid it well. 'Of course. We can do it now, if you'd like.'

Sam smiled. She thought it was cute Kiefel thought she had a choice. 'That would be good.' She about turned and led the way down the corridor.

'I'm not sure if you witnessed what just happened,' Kiefel said, aware that there were cameras in every room which Sam could tap into at any given minute. Seeing as the alarms had gone off, there was no way Sam wouldn't have logged on to see what was happening.

'I did.'

'I thought it might be a good idea to let it play out instead of starting again, given how far they've come this time around.'

'A sensible decision.'

Kiefel, walking a few steps behind Sam, frowned. She'd thought the impromptu "meeting" was about what had happened in the room. From her reaction, she clearly wasn't bothered. 'Can I ask what you wanted to see me about?'

Sam smirked. 'I don't know. *Can* you?'

A flashback to her school days; Kiefel could remember her teachers picking her up for the same grammatical error. It had irritated her then; it irritated her now. But - like being at school - she couldn't say anything. It was just the teacher / boss asserting their dominance. 'May I ask what you wanted to see me about?'

'You may…'

There was an elevator at the end of the corridor. Sam pressed the call button and waited for the doors to open. She didn't have long to wait. She gestured for Kiefel to proceed which she duly did. Sam stepped in and pressed the button for the top floor. The doors closed and the elevator jolted as it started its journey.

'How long have we been running these experiments for?'

'From working on the serum?'

Sam laughed. 'No. Just the human trial part will do.'

Kiefel shrugged. Off the top of her head, she didn't know the exact timeframe. 'A year or so?'

'And how much progress has been made?'

'We continue to make progress with each…'

Sam cut her off. 'Not what I asked. I asked *how much* progress has been made?' Before Kiefel had a chance to answer, Sam continued, 'I'll tell you: Not enough. Every day I have people breathing down my neck and every day I have to break the news that we haven't got a product for them. Needless to say, they are getting frustrated. *Needless* to say, *I* am getting frustrated.'

The elevator doors opened. Sam stepped out and continued down yet another long corridor. It led to her office with fine art hanging on either side of the walls. Just one picture was worth more than what any of the doctors here earned on an annual basis and yet here they were, hidden away from the eyes of those who never got to come up to this floor.

Sam used her keycard to open the office door.

Kiefel was surprised to see another woman waiting on the other side of the doors. She was seated at Sam's desk, with an empty seat beside her.

Sam continued the previous conversation from the corridor, 'And needless to say, when I am frustrated, changes must be made.' She gestured towards the other woman who, in turn, got up and extended her hand towards Kiefel. 'This is Dr. Tiffany Howard. From here on in, she will be overseeing the project.'

'Pleasure to make your acquaintance,' Dr. Howard said, a broad smile on her face.

'Pleased to meet you,' Kiefel said, unsure what any of this meant for her own job. She turned to Sam, hoping to be put out of her misery with regards to what was going on.

'You're not losing your job,' Sam said. 'I acknowledge you've been a credit to the corporation but, at the same time, we need results and, at present, you're not delivering. This is merely a shake-up. You will still oversee the staff downstairs, but you will be reporting directly to Dr. Howard.'

'I see.'

'Now obviously because you're no longer doing the same tasks, this does mean there will be a restructuring in the pay.'

'Of course. I understand,' Kiefel said, swallowing her rage.

'I will email you the specifics and give you the rest of the day to decide whether you wish to continue your employment here or look elsewhere. Obviously I hope you continue on with us but fully understand...'

Kiefel cut her off, 'I'm sure it will be fine.'

'That's the spirit.' Sam smiled. 'Well, if you can show Dr. Howard her office and bring her up to speed with today's events, I would be very grateful.'

Kiefel turned to Dr. Howard. 'Do you know where your office is? I'll be happy to show you.'

'She will be in your office,' Sam said. 'The staff know that's the management office, so it makes sense to keep things as they are. We will provide you a work station in the open plan offices.'

'Of course. Makes perfect sense.' Kiefel forced a smile. 'Well then... Are you ready to see your office?'

'If now's a good time for you,' Dr. Howard said.

Chapter Eighteen

'Come to spy on us?' Dr. Ashley Chmielewski couldn't hide the smirk on her face when she saw Dr. Kiefel setting up her new office space in the communal area, along with the other doctors.

Having shown Dr. Howard to her new office, Kiefel had gone to set up her own work space. 'If we want progress, it's fair to say we have to work closer together,' Kiefel said, not wanting to admit she'd been demoted to someone who was, for all intents and purposes, beneath her. What she didn't know was that an email had already been sent around the team, explaining the change in management.

Another person, sitting close by, who was unable to hide her smile was Dr. Schwartz. She'd had it in for Kiefel ever since she'd tried to help one of the test subjects as they had a seizure. Instead of calling Schwartz into the office and explaining the process to her again, she berated her in front of everyone; unnecessarily embarrassing her over something which could have been handled much more discreetly. Kiefel had gone on to say that it was a "lesson for everyone" and how she was lucky she still had a job. From that day, even if Schwartz saw Kiefel and wished her a good morning, she was ignored. When staff received bonus payments, she was also shunned. It was nice to see Kiefel experience she same kind of treatment she'd been so willing to dish out to others. Schwartz's only regret was she hadn't been dismissed because the atmosphere would have definitely been less frosty if she were gone.

With the smile seemingly frozen on her smug face, Schwartz said, 'Sorry to hear about the demotion.' The moment the words left her mouth, the room fell silent. All eyes turned to Kiefel, curious to see how she'd react. Schwartz didn't care. She carried on, 'I was shocked when we all got the email. Still at least your conversation took place in private.'

Kiefel smiled. 'We roll with the punches.' She continued setting her desk space up while wishing, back when Schwartz had gone against the training provided, she'd just kicked her to the curb there and then. To change the subject and stop from biting back to Schwartz, Kiefel asked Dr. Chmielewski, 'How were the test subjects when you left them?'

'On their own beds sitting in silence.' Chmielewski added, 'I think with the rising tension, it might be a good idea to separate them. At the moment she seems to be compliant to what we're asking but I'm not sure how long that will last if he is there dripping poison in her ear.'

Ever since the husband and wife duo of Mark and Sophia Flemmich had gone sour, there'd been calls to have experiments kept to one person per room. They had been pushed to the side given the lack of space and *need* to test more than one individual at a time. With each experiment, more than one patient was given the serum to rule out an allergic reaction being the cause of it failing. For example: If one person had a seizure and died, was it because of the serum itself *or* because they were allergic to it? Another test would need to be set up with another patient to determine the answer which then stretched the experiment to at least double the time. If both subjects were set up together and passed from the same cause, chances were it was the serum, and the company could move on to the next batch.

'We don't have the space for that,' Kiefel said.

'I know that's usually the case but given that they've lasted longer than previous tests, I'm just thinking it might be worthwhile *making* the space on this occasion.'

What Chmielewski said made sense but, after the demotion, the last thing Kiefel was going to do was go and highlight to Sam that someone else had made a valid point. She already had the final nail primed, ready for the coffin that was her career. Having someone beneath her then step over her with a suggestion she really should have considered herself would have been the last blow needed. If only to get Dr. Chmielewski off her back, Kiefel said, 'If you're concerned about them, increase the security outside their room and ensure the viewing area is never left vacant. We have the manpower to see to it they're monitored twenty-four-seven so make sure it's done.'

Chmielewski didn't bother to argue. It was clear from Kiefel's tone that she wasn't in the mood to discuss anything. She got up from her desk and made her way back to the viewing room to put the guards in place and continue the close monitoring of what could be the last stages of the experiment.

Kiefel called after her, 'I believe we have a Mr. Lucas Wilson starting with security today. You can station him there alongside the current guard.'

Before stepping through the door, Chmielewski said, 'I'll call for him and get him sent up.' With that, she stepped from the open plan office and continued through the network of winding corridors.

As Kiefel finished setting up her new office space, her watch sounded with a reminder's alarm. She didn't need to look at it to know what it was trying to remind her about; there was a meeting scheduled with a representative from the government. She dismissed the alarm and went to make her way to the meeting room only to hesitate a moment. With all that had happened with her current role, she wasn't sure if she was still in line to run the meeting or whether that had also been handed over to Dr. Howard. She continued to head for the meeting. If she didn't go and *was* still running it, she'd be in trouble. If she went and wasn't needed, it might have been embarrassing but at least she could still sit in on the conversation. While she wasn't the top of the food chain anymore, she was still within the management sector and would still need to be feeding back the outcome of the meeting to those beneath her.

Aware the meeting was happening, Schwartz called out, 'Good luck.' Given Schwartz had taken the experiment over after Dr. Chappo's demise, she already knew Dr. Howard was leading the meeting; it had become evident after Howard had gone through all the various tests with her, gathering as much information as she possibly could ahead of the presentation. Still, she wasn't about to let Kiefel know this. Her thought process being "fuck her" as it would be more embarrassing to see the extent of how much she'd been replaced in a room full of senior management and those she was supposed to be presenting to.

Kiefel ignored her false well wishes.

Part Five
Before

Chapter Nineteen

Dr. Schwartz sat opposite Dr. Kiefel and Sam Schlecht in a state of shock. Kiefel was leading the meeting with Sam watching from the side-lines. It had been a day since the *creature* had pulled Dr. Chappo's head off before being gunned down with a full clip of ammo from a guard's assault rifle and while the sound of gunfire had echoed through the back corridors, until now no one *really* knew what had happened to Dr. Chappo. At least, no one in any of the higher up positions. Such was the depth to which the news was buried, this was the first Schwartz was hearing about it and, even then, it was more of a need to know situation as opposed to simply informing her a colleague had passed.

Kiefel had first broken the news that Dr. Chappo was dead and then explained how he'd come to pass, telling Schwartz about the creature which had crawled from one of the test subject's warm corpses. She went on to explain that there was potential for a little side project with what Dr. Chappo had discovered hatching from within the dead body and, with him no longer able to lead the program, that they'd need someone to take over with his experiments. That person, Kiefel explained, would be Dr. Schwartz.

To Schwartz it made it sound like a step up the metaphorical ladder within the workplace; a chance to lead her own set of experiments. To Kiefel, it was a way of getting Schwartz off the more important project and boxed into a small room. She was still dubious it could lead to anything and, when it didn't, she'd have the perfect excuse to let Schwartz go given there'd be no further use for her, given the time it would take her to get up to speed with the main project they'd been working on.

More or less using Dr. Chappo's words, Kiefel explained, 'There's potential here to give our soldiers on the front line another chance if they happen to die in battle. Imagine it, they're killed in the line of action and from their corpse, another version of them grows out. With one simple injection, we can double the size of our army with no further recruitment. Each life will be worth two and - the second life? It took a full round of ammunition to kill it so... Also, stronger than the person it grew from.'

The appearance of the "second life" didn't matter to Kiefel and, in discussion with Sam, it didn't matter to her either. All that mattered was that they got the serum stable enough to not induce a seizure in those who took it. It was entirely necessary for the users to live as normal life as possible until the day they died and, from there onwards. The perfect death would be in battle but, if they died of natural causes or anything outside of a battleground, it could be dealt with by incinerating the corpses before anything had a chance to come crawling out. This was obviously a big ask of soldiers who wished to be buried as opposed to cremated but that was a bridge they could cross once they'd developed a fully-working serum and once it was approved for use amongst those in service. For now, the biggest challenge they faced was to get something stable enough to present to those who might have an interest in such a formula.

Kiefel explained that it would be a skeleton crew working around the clock on the second formula. Their main task was still in the other department, one which could be sold to the masses, and - as such - resources would be limited. There'd be one experiment at a time and the budget for said experiment would not be as high as that used elsewhere. Schwartz didn't care. She couldn't see that she was being side-lined. To her, it was an exciting chance to work on something new. A possibility to prove herself worthy within the company and, from there, she could ask for higher wages and further opportunities then.

'So would this be of interest?'

Without hesitation, Schwartz answered, 'Yes.' She quickly added, 'And thank you for the opportunity.'

Kiefel turned to Sam on the off-chance she wanted to add anything further. She didn't say anything. Unlike Kiefel, and Dr. Chappo before he died, Sam wasn't entirely convinced about the additional experiments. They were already behind where she wanted to be with the main one so, to her, it was nothing more than an unnecessary distraction. The only reason she was "okay" for it to proceed was because it had been guaranteed to be run with a skeleton crew, wouldn't *really* cost anything additional and *did* have the potential to bring in more money *if* it was successful. What she hadn't said was that she'd give it six months. If no progress had been made within that timeframe, she'd pull the plug.

When it was clear Sam had nothing else to add, Kiefel turned back to Dr. Schwartz and said, 'Well, unless you have any questions, I'll show you the video Dr. Chappo took, and we can go about setting things in motion.' She asked, 'Do you have any additional questions?'

Dr. Schwartz resisted the urge to ask if there'd be a pay-rise with this change in responsibilities. 'No. I think I'm good.'

'Well, that's that then,' Kiefel said. She stood up and extended her hand towards Schwartz. She also stood before shaking Kiefel's hand, unaware she'd pretty much guaranteed her future redundancy.

Chapter Twenty

The footage taken from the autopsy was shocking to watch; the dead body split from naval to the top of the head with this *thing* within, trying to reach out for a freedom it couldn't yet grasp. Dr. Schwartz watched with a mixture of horror and morbid fascination as Kiefel hovered close behind. 'Needless to say, as with everything else we do here, this is highly confidential. I do not want you speaking of this to anyone not directly involved in what you're working on.'

Schwartz said, 'I wouldn't even know *how* to explain this even if I wanted to.'

'Dr. Chappo's idea was to see where this would lead. Was it an anomaly or was it something that could be replicated? Furthermore, what would happen if left it to grow? As you saw from the video it was growing fast in just the short time we were together and... *As we also know* it grew more from there too; eventually pulling itself free and taking Dr. Chappo's life.' She continued, 'Now if this *is* something that can be replicated and if we *can* give those who take the serum a full and healthy life ahead of this growing from them... There's a good chance we could sell it to the military. Think of it as a kind of biological weapon.'

'I can see it.'

'There's great potential here..'

Schwartz nodded. 'I can see *that* too.'

'Whether it's possible... Who knows but it's something Dr. Chappo was keen to explore on the side and, well, it would be nice if his death wasn't entirely in vain.' For a moment, Schwartz almost believed Kiefel cared but she knew better. For Dr. Kiefel, it was all about the potential money to be made and anything else was just a smokescreen to try and make her appear more human.

Keen for Schwartz to see the whole picture, Kiefel leaned across her and loaded up another file on the computer; footage caught through the two-way mirror which showed Dr. Chappo's final moments. 'I warn you,' she said, 'this is fairly graphic.' She hit play and stepped to the side so as not to block Schwartz's view. Schwartz watched in horror as the creature pulled itself free from the dead body ahead of lunging for Chappo. Such was the suddenness of the attack; he had no time to try and defend himself or jump from its path. It was over within a couple of seconds, which was, for Chappo at least, a blessing. The room's lighting turned red, and an alarm rang out, blasting through the computer's tinny speakers. Kiefel leaned forward and stopped the playback if only to silence the alarm.

'I would suggest caution with the next subject you try this on. Once it's in the room, I wouldn't put anyone else in there if and when the insides hatch out. Monitor only through the viewing room. When it comes to feeding…' Kiefel's voice trailed off. She had no idea what these things ate or if they even felt hunger the same way as a normal person would. 'Well, if anything needs to be put into the room, I suggest using one of the rooms that has a hatch in the doorway.'

'No. No. I'll be careful. I understand.'

'Good.' Kiefel smiled. 'We don't need any more unnecessary paperwork and pay-offs to grieving families.' And that was how she *really* felt about Chappo's untimely demise.

'Do we have any subjects ready for this?'

Kiefel slid a file across the table. 'Ariel Kollmansberger. Might as well start with one where we know the body produces the creature.' She continued, 'Ariel's not quite ready yet. She's still cooking but - should only be a few more days. As for the serum, we're using some of that and some of the next batch… We *think* we have eliminated the problem of the seizures but, obviously, time will tell.'

Schwartz said, 'Sounds like you've pretty much taken care of things already.'

'We had to keep the ball rolling while we decided what to do. From here on in, it's all up to you.'

'I might go down to the labs and see how far along Ariel is.'

'Can't hurt. I did tell them we were in a hurry so…'

'And if she's not ready? What do I do then given everything else is taken care of? Is the room set up?'

'The room is set up, yes. If she's not ready, I guess you get a half-day today. Lucky you.'

Schwartz smiled. 'It is my lucky day, huh.'

'You can make the hours up when the experiment gets going properly,' Kiefel added. Schwartz laughed even though she knew her manager wasn't joking.

'Okay, well, I'm going to go and check on Ariel,' Schwartz said. She pushed herself away from the desk and stood up. Kiefel didn't bother showing her to the door; Dr. Schwartz knew the way. Instead, she sat down in the very same chair Schwartz had just evacuated. 'I'll let you know how it goes,' Schwartz said as she stepped from the room.

Chapter Twenty-one

Schwartz normally stayed away from the "cooking room". It wasn't it's proper name, just a nick-name the staff had given it due to what took place within, and Schwartz wasn't the only one who liked to put distance between the room and herself. The biggest complaints the staff had being both the smell (burned rubber) and that the bodies in early-growth freaked them out.

The bodies, set beneath large heat lamps and with a multiple of IV drips plugged into different parts of their limbs, were laid out on tables. They started the cycle as white puddles which, as the days went on, slowly started to take a more human form, albeit with an almost translucent jelly-like appearance to their skin. As they neared completion, these skin tones became the natural colour of whoever was growing at the time.

Ariel was currently translucent. Her human shape had taken form but her "skin" was still slimy and wet. It was this moistness which gave off the burnt smell of rubber as it slowly cooked beneath the lamps.

'How's she coming along?' Schwartz knew nothing about the process involved in cooking up the test subjects. For all she knew Ariel was in the final process and it wouldn't take much longer but why second guess things?

Dr. Henderson was working in the cooking room. After what had happened to her previous test subjects, Mark and Sophia Flemmich, it was decided she'd be better suited in another department where the job at hand was more straightforward. She glanced across to the form on the table before having a quick look through a file which she pulled from a small cradle at the end of Ariel's table. 'On track for tomorrow, I believe.'

'So, I'm not needed today then. Okay, that's great.'

'Not sure why we're cooking up a fresh batch,' Henderson continued, 'it's not as though we have had much joy with this batch before.'

Schwartz smiled. She'd already been warned to keep the details of this experiment secret and, given Henderson's reaction, it was clear the team here knew nothing about what was going on. 'Maybe we'll get luckier with this one.'

'Just a waste of time if you ask me.'

There were two more bodies on tables next to Ariel which were closer to completion. James and Emily. While Schwartz found the whole process creepy, she still couldn't help but be impressed with how close to the real thing these subjects became once they were fully grown. If it weren't for the colouring of the insides, a person would be hard pressed to see the difference between these and the real thing. 'I don't recognise these two.'

'Fresh in,' Henderson said.

'Exciting.' She asked, 'Are they related too?'

'Nope. Strangers. Again, if you ask me it's a mistake putting them in together, but my opinion counts for nothing. I'm just a cook now.'

'Well at least you still have a job,' Schwartz said. With the failure of the last experiment, Henderson could just as easily been fired.

A weird thing to say, Henderson thought. 'Always good to have a job,' Henderson said. She knew better than to sound ungrateful for her role. One thing she'd come to learn about the corporation was that there were many snakes within the company and if these *snakes* had a way to step on someone to further their own career, they'd take it.

Emily's body suddenly twitched as her left leg kicked out. Another of the doctors was quick to check the machines monitoring her. 'Oh shit. I think she's waking up.'

Henderson acted fast. She hurried across the room to a medical cabinet and promptly filled a syringe with a high-powered sedative before rushing over to where Emily continued to stir. She stabbed the needle into Emily's arm and emptied the sedative into her veins. As per the plan, Emily's body stopped twitching.

The other doctor asked, 'Do you think we should give the guy the same amount to ensure they wake at similar times?'

'No. It's fine,' Henderson said. 'Just get them taken to their rooms as quickly as possible. They're ready to go down anyway.'

The other doctor nodded and reached for a phone which hung from the wall. A quick call to the porter and James and Emily would be collected and wheeled down to their new home.

'I can see you're busy,' Schwartz said. 'I only came to check on the progress of Ariel.' On the off-chance the cooking process was over faster than anticipated, she said, 'When she's ready, if I'm not back in the building, just call my mobile. I only live about twenty minutes from here, so it won't take long to get back.'

'Will do,' Henderson said.

Having seen enough, Schwartz left the room. The first thing she did, as she stepped out into the corridor, was to take a deep lungful of fresher air. She had no idea how the cooks worked in that stuffy room; a situation made worse with the lack of ventilation in there. Still, she shrugged the stink off, it wasn't her problem. In fact, whatever else happened here for the rest of the day wasn't "her problem". Kiefel said to make the time up so, for now, she'd make the most of her unexpected freedom.

* * * * *

Chapter One

He watched from across the room. She was sleeping soundly; quiet little snores which brought him some comfort despite his predicament. *Naked*, just as he was.

It took everything not to call across and wake her. The only reason he didn't being that, with her sleeping, he was safe from whatever *this* was. Was she a part of it? Was it her who, somehow, brought him to this room? Was she the one who had removed his clothes and hidden them. No. Ridiculous. It couldn't have been her. At least, certainly not by herself.

She was in her thirties. A pretty woman; blonde hair, and a slight frame. With her laying down on the other single bed in the white room, he could only guess her height. Five foot five? He was bulky, muscular. Six foot two. There was no way she could have brought him to this place by herself. But then, if she had an accomplice, how come there was no one else in here?

She started to stir. His heart skipped a beat. *This is it.* Her eyes opened and immediately squinted against the harsh fluorescent lights. Only once comfortable to do so did they open fully and -

\- *immediate* panic.

Part Six
Today

Chapter Twenty-two

Henry Phillips greeted Sam with a firm handshake and a "good morning". She introduced him to Dr. Howard who'd be leading the meeting and showing their results. With formal introductions done, he took the seat offered to him.

Henry Phillips worked for the Ministry of Defence. While he didn't know exactly what he was about to be shown, the emails and calls had been sufficient for him to come down to the main office to see what was on offer.

Dr. Howard had already set up a projector to show the footage they'd prepared, showcasing different parts of the experiment they'd been working on, along with detailed reports of their findings. For this meeting, they'd removed the part of the footage which showed Dr. Chappo having his head pulled from his body; it wasn't exactly a good advert.

Instead of starting with a long speech about what they'd been trying to achieve with their experimentation, Dr. Howard simply said, 'I think the best thing we can do is show you footage of what we're offering. From there, you're free to ask questions and we can go more in-depth into things. Is that okay with you?'

Henry agreed, 'If that's what you think.' With a smile, he added, 'I'm just here for the show and tell so, sure… Show me.'

There was a knock on the door. Sam looked up, 'Come in?'

The door opened and Kiefel appeared. She immediately saw Dr. Howard at the front of the board room, standing next to the projector's screen and knew she wasn't needed. 'Sorry, I wasn't sure if you still needed me?'

Sam glanced over to Dr. Howard. 'Do you have everything you need?'

With a forced smile on her face, Howard said, 'I think we're good, thank you.' She realised it was weird to have another staff member burst in at the start of a meeting so explained, 'This is Dr. Kiefel. She used to head the program until recent changes.'

Henry Phillips momentarily stood, extending his hand towards Kiefel. 'Pleasure to meet you.'

Kiefel smiled but, inside, she was dying. 'And you.'

Keen to get the meeting underway, Sam dismissed Kiefel, 'Well thank you for stopping by but as you can see, everything's under control. If we need you, we'll call down.'

'Of course. Not a problem.' Kiefel stepped from the room, closing the door behind her. The last thing she heard from the room was Dr. Howard apologising for the interruption, promptly followed by Henry stating it was nice to see the staff were all keen and helpful.

Kiefel made her way down the corridor. With every step she could feel her blood pumping furiously. *The staff*? The main experiment, the whole purpose of what they've been trying to do, might well be lagging behind the planned schedule but she'd been as much a part in the side project; certainly, more so than Dr. Howard who'd just walked in to claim all the glory. Usually, when feeling the frustration of the working environment, she'd go to her office and hide away until she'd calmed but that wasn't possible with where her new office was located. Especially with Dr. Schwartz sitting at her desk with that self-satisfied, shit-eating grin plastered on her face. If she went down there now, she could clearly envision herself hitting Schwartz straight in her smug face and while there was no denying it wouldn't be satisfying, it probably wouldn't help her get her old job back.

As Kiefel turned the next corner, she almost bumped directly into Dr. Chmielewski who, instead of apologising for almost knocking her manager over, quickly said, 'Thank God. I've been calling your phone…'

'You have?' Kiefel reached into the pocket of her laboratory coat. Sure enough, there were a number of missed calls. 'What is it?' From the look on Chmielewski's face, it clearly wasn't "good" news.

'You need to come and see this.' Aware the walls had ears, it wasn't sensible to talk about the experiment outside of the monitoring rooms or the white rooms themselves. She about turned and led the way with Kiefel close behind, wondering what else could possibly go wrong. She promptly pushed the thought from her mind. With the way things had already gone today, she really didn't need to tempt fate. She knew, from experience, things could *always* get worse.

Not wanting to wait until they got to the white room, Kiefel cut to the chase and asked, 'Tell me we haven't lost them?'

'They're still alive,' Chmielewski said.

That was something at least.

Chmielewski continued, 'But I don't think we can leave them in there. We're going to need to separate them before things get further out of hand.'

Kiefel was almost afraid to ask, 'Almost?'

'You just need to see for yourself.'

Chapter Twenty-three

'What did you want us to do?' Chmielewski asked after giving Kiefel a moment to see what had happened in the time since she'd last been in the viewing room.

'Is that what I think it is?' A rhetorical question. Kiefel knew what it was as there was nothing else in the room it *could* have been.

James had defected into his hand and smeared it onto the mirror. His intentions were obvious; to block the view of those watching through the two-way mirror. Unable to see, they'd be forced to go into the room and, from there, he'd probably be waiting to try and break free. Speculation of course given he'd not made any of his plans known. He simply shit and wiped. With the mirror as large as it was, it would take more than one "emptying" to fully cover it, but the intentions were definitely clear.

Kiefel asked, 'What about her? What has she done through all of this?'

Emily was still sitting on her bed. She had her hand pressed to her mouth and nose in an effort to stop the stench, not that it was helping given the expression of pure disgust on her face.

Chmielewski continued, 'If we leave them in the room together, I can't see it having the ending we're hoping for.'

Kiefel hesitated a moment. The way she saw it, there were three choices ahead of her. The first was that she could leave them in the room together and force them to go through to the end of the experiment, or as long as this serum permitted at least - seeing as there were no guarantees *this* was the one that wouldn't have any problems. The second choice was to split them up and put them in their own room. If James wanted to be disruptive then his actions would only impact him while they'd still have Emily doing all that they asked in order to get the call home; the call which would never be permitted. The third option, something they'd never tried before, was to tell them the truth about their situation.

Due to the way that the experiment was put together, the truth awaited all those who survived until the end of the tests. The subjects would never be released but it only seemed fair to let them know the part they'd played in making the world an *easier* place, for those who could afford it, before the experiment was terminated. Maybe there was a benefit in telling those within the white room about what was happening though? Perhaps, when they realised how important this was, they'd be more happy to go along with what was being asked of them and they wouldn't fight back? It was something which, until now, hadn't been considered but at this stage, with James literally smearing shit on the mirror to stop himself from being monitored, what did they have to lose?

Seeing Kiefel was in deep thought, Chmielewski asked, 'What are you thinking?'

As far as Kiefel was concerned, this wasn't a conversation to be had with Chmielewski. This was something to discuss with... Who? Previously she would have gone straight to Sam with such thoughts but what now? Was she supposed to go to Dr. Howard? And what then? If Dr. Howard thought it a bad idea, there was a chance she could discuss her frustrations with Sam behind Kiefel's back, possibly making the situation worse than it sounded. And if it was a good idea? She'd take credit for it and Kiefel wouldn't get the recognition she deserved. 'Just thinking,' Kiefel said. 'I think, for now, we should separate them.'

The temporary plan meant there'd be one less room for the other experiments but, coming this far with these two, it was worth sacrificing some space. The move also meant she could buy herself a little time to think about what she *really* wanted to do with them; another thought being that it would be better to simply cut their losses with the man and put him down now so as to concentrate on the woman. At least this way they could see whether the body could go on to grow a *second life* like the others. They were pretty much sure they'd already eliminated that problem already but what would it hurt to do one more investigation if they had a body going spare?

Kiefel continued, 'You put the new guard on the door too?'

Dr. Chmielewski nodded. 'Yes.'

'Okay so we'll take the woman from this room and put her elsewhere. Give her the new guard as it's a fair assumption to say that it will be an easier task for him to deal with. Keep the man in this room, he can put up with the stink of his own mess. The more experienced guard to be left here if things do take a downward turn.'

Chmielewski asked, 'And what constitutes a "downward" turn exactly?' In her eyes, the downward turned had already happened the moment James started smearing shit on the mirror.

'If he gets violent, if he tries to break out… Make it clear, I want the program terminated.'

'And should it come down to that do we get another set up?'

'No. We will wait and see how it plays out with the woman. By the time we've cooked up another subject and got them underway, we might already have all the answers needed from her. If things fall foul with her and the seizures come back, we know we need to start afresh with another serum. For now, though, it's *his* mind that has gone and that's a human problem as opposed to anything we've done.' Kiefel also knew that this "problem" was on them too, not just *his* mind. There'd been promises of rewards if the subjects played their part but other than decent food, so far, there'd been given nothing. It was only ever going to be a matter of time before their minds snapped from the boredom and frustration of being trapped within the white room. There was a part of Kiefel which was surprised it had taken this long; she would have snapped much sooner had the shoe been on the other foot.

'And I write all this in the report?'

'Yes. But I'll also be speaking to Sam,' Kiefel said. Since having her initial thoughts about how to handle this, she'd already decided that the best course of action would be to approach her for herself; let her know she would be splitting the couple up, let her know she would be terminating the male subject should it come down to it and even questioning whether it would be worth telling them the truth about their situation. It would be a conversation she'd be having as soon as the meeting with the gentleman from the M.O.D was finished.

Chmielewski understood the assignment. 'We'll get the woman moved.'

'Perfect.' Kiefel didn't need to stand around watching the instructions being followed. They were simply enough. She went to leave the room to return to her "office" knowing that, once the meeting was over, Dr. Howard and Sam would be passing through to get to their own offices. Once she saw them, she'd wait for Dr. Howard to turn off and then run after Sam. In her head, a simple enough plan, she'd have her old job back before the end of the week. She paused as a thought ran through her mind. 'Oh, and give the woman an iPad. The nurse can stay with her but, let her record a video message. We don't need to send it, but it might be enough to let her know we're listening…' Such a simple idea that Kiefel didn't understand why she'd not thought of it before. 'Just make sure you don't leave the iPad with her. Get the guard to wait with her.'

Chmielewski nodded again. 'Not a problem.'

With that, Kiefel left the room and made her way back to her new office space while Chmielewski reached for the walkie-talkie to prep the guards and get Kiefel's instructions underway.

Chapter Twenty-four

Henry Phillips shook hands with Dr. Howard first and then Sam. After watching the presentation and hearing what was offered, he was suitably impressed but cautious about agreeing anything without first talking to the rest of the board. Unless the serum was something which could be administered on the quiet, he couldn't see the average person willingly sign up to receiving anything which meant they came back as a *form* of who they were before. In fact, he could see a large uproar if the general public got hold of the information. That wasn't to say they wouldn't go ahead with making a deal to use it - it wouldn't be the first time they'd experimented on soldiers - but, if they did, they'd need to tread *very* carefully. 'You've given us a lot to think about,' he said.

Dr. Howard pushed, 'If you have any questions or concerns, please do not hesitate to get in touch. We can arrange another meeting in-person or do it via a video call if easier.'

'Well, we will definitely be in touch to let you know our thoughts,' he said.

Sam smiled, quietly confident the program *would* be of interest to the Ministry of Defence. 'We'll wait to hear from you,' she said. And, if for some reason it wasn't for them? There were plenty of other organisations she could approach, even ones from overseas. 'I'll walk you out,' she added.

'That's great. Thank you.'

Sam led Henry from the room. Dr. Howard breathed a sigh of relief. *Nothing like being thrown in the deep end.* Given she hadn't had much time to prepare for the meeting, she figured she handled it as well as she could have and, like Sam, was fairly confident a deal would be made. And if it was? It would be an easy victory for her to claim despite not being part of the program until the very end.

Quietly she started to pack everything away.

As Sam walked Henry to the exit he asked, 'So what else are you working on here?'

Sam wasn't in the business of giving details away. To avoid having to go into things, she simply said, 'We have our fingers in many pies.'

'I bet you do.' Henry knew she wasn't about to give anything up so easily but figured it had been worth a try. 'Well, if there's anything else you think may be of interest to us…'

'You'll be the first port of call,' Sam lied. In reality, the "first port of call" was actually for those who had the deepest pockets and despite the government's wealth, those pockets usually belonged to private individuals who'd be willing to pay anything for results without trying to negotiate a better price. The government had spending power for sure, but that didn't mean they wouldn't try and get the price down before any deals were made. Sam didn't mind offering this serum to them because, at the end of the day, it had been a "lucky mistake".

They reached the main reception area. Henry reached into his pocket and pulled out a business card. He handed it over to Sam as he told her, 'Like I said, if there's anything else you think might be of interest to us… This is my direct number and personal email so, cut the middle man out and come straight to me.'

'That's perfect,' Sam said as she took the card.

'And we'll be in touch soon.' He hesitated. 'I… take it we're the only ones to have been offered this opportunity so far?'

'That's right, yes.'

'If you can keep it like that for the next seventy-two hours I'd be grateful.'

Sam smiled. She knew he was well and truly on the hook. 'Of course.' She extended her hand for a second time.

With a smile, he took her hand in his and they shook. Henry pulled away. 'We'll talk soon.' He turned and headed for the exit. Sam watched until he left the building before she turned to the receptionist and gave the woman an excited thumbs up. The receptionist had no idea what the meeting had been about but, if the CEO was happy - it could only be good news. She smiled back as Sam disappeared into the main part of the building.

'Sam, may I have a word with you?'

Sam had barely set foot into the corridor when Kiefel made her approach.

'Now's not the best time,' Sam said. She wasn't lying. With a morning tied up with a meeting, she knew there'd be other tasks to catch up on. She also didn't really want to have further discussions with Dr. Kiefel given she presumed it would be in reference to the demotion.

'I'm afraid it's not something that can wait,' Kiefel pushed. 'It's about the test subjects…'

Sam stopped in her tracks. She turned to face Kiefel. 'The test subjects?'

'Yes. There's been a problem. They're both still okay but…'

'And why are you bringing it to my attention?'

'Because…'

'Your first port of call should be Dr. Howard. I thought that was made obvious this morning? You report to her and, if it needs my attention, she will come to me.'

'But…'

'Unless you're saying you're not willing to accept your new position in which case…'

'No. I'm fine with the new position. I just thought that, given I have been running these experiments for so long, on this occasion it would be better to come direct to you. So as to give Dr. Howard time to settle…' Kiefel had to tread carefully. If she pushed too hard, she knew she'd lost the job.

'Dr. Howard is more than competent and has been fully brought up to speed with everything involved. Like I said, if you have any concerns, thoughts, problems, successes - everything needs to go through her. Understood?'

'Yes.'

'Good.'

If only to end their run-in on a more positive note, Kiefel asked, 'How was the meeting?'

Sam ignored her. As far as she was concerned, Kiefel wasn't a part of that team anymore, so it was none of her business. She turned her back on her and walked away, calmly saying, 'A memo will be sent out when we're ready to make any announcements.'

Kiefel didn't follow. She stayed, rooted to the spot - that bubbling hatred continually simmering away. For all the years she's given the company, for all the work she'd put in - this was how it was going to go now? To hell with telling Dr. Howard. She'd been running the experiment since day one. She didn't need to go to anyone else to discuss her thoughts. She'd just push on and make an executive decision for herself. 'Fuck them.' She said again, more determination this time, '*Fuck* them.' Kiefel wasn't the only one who was growing tired with the way the corporation had been running its shady business practises.

Lucas had also had enough and had been feeling this way long before accepting a job as a guard. He wasn't there to *guard* anything. He was there to bring the corporation down from within.

Chapter Twenty-five

Emily stepped into her new room.. This room was more or less the same; the only real notable differences being the size; it was smaller, with only one bed. There was still a single toilet and two-way mirror so she could be watched from beyond. While it wasn't the freedom she'd been hoping for, when first pulled from her last "home", she was still grateful to be split up from James. Especially after he'd continued mouthing off, shouting abuse, to the guards as they came to get her. One guard stayed with James, positioning himself outside the door while the second one, Lucas Wilson, walked escorted Emily. As she cast her eyes around the room, he said, 'This will be your room from now on.'

Relieved to be away from James, Emily simply said, 'Thank you.'

Lucas wasn't done. He had an iPad tucked under his arm. He took it in his hand and held it towards her. 'This is for you too.'

'What's this?'

'They've said you can record the message for your daughter.'

Emily hesitated, unsure whether this was a trap or not. 'I can?'

Lucas nodded. 'That's what I've been told.'

Emily took the iPad from him. She looked at it. It was already powered-on, ready to be used. She laughed. 'I don't know what to say now,' she said. 'Do I get time to think about it?'

'I'm afraid not. You need to record your message now and then; I have to take it away again.'

'I see.' Her heart sank when she realised she wasn't even getting any privacy to record it. Whatever she had to say, it was to be done in front of him. 'Now?' Lucas nodded.

Emily took the iPad over to the bed. She sat herself down and loaded up the camera. Despite having the mirror in the other room, she'd not paid much attention to her reflection. The sight of herself using the tablet's camera shocked her. She'd lost weight; her face was gaunt, her hair greasy and there were dark bags hanging under her eyes. Trying to make light of the situation, she said, 'Supposed to stop my daughter from worrying… Not sure the sight of me will help with that.' She glanced up to Lucas and asked, 'Don't suppose you have a bag of make-up hidden anywhere, do you?'

Lucas solemnly shook his head. 'I'm afraid not.'

'I know. I was just being silly.' She looked at the tablet again. 'I wish I knew what to say to make it so she wouldn't worry.'

'It really doesn't matter.'

The way Lucas spoke; Emily knew his words were loaded with double meaning. Her heart sank. 'They're not going to show it to her, are they?'

Lucas stepped forward and put his back to the mirror so his mouth couldn't be seen. 'They can't show her anything you film,' he said. He spoke in a hushed voice which was barely audible to Emily, let alone anyone watching from behind the mirror and he knew they *would* be watching and they *would* be listening. 'Don't look at me,' he said quickly in the same hushed tone. 'Pretend you're looking at the screen, thinking about what you're going to say.'

Confused, Emily did as she was told.

'You're not a real person,' he said. 'You're a clone of the person you used to be. You're here because you died and they'd done a deal, buying fresh corpses from the morgues to harvest the DNA. I know this is a lot to take in but as far as your daughter is aware, you're dead. The real you died in a car crash on the way to get your daughter from school… I know it all sounds crazy and hard to believe but I promise you I'm telling you the truth. They will *never* let you talk to your daughter, and they will *never* let you out of here. You're nothing more than an expendable experiment.'

Emily just sat there. Even if she could get away with looking him in the eye and having a proper conversation with him, she had no idea what she'd say to him. What *was* she supposed to say to something like that? Something so *unbelievable*?

'Just know,' he said, 'that there's a group of us working on trying to free you. Trying to bring this whole thing burning down to the ground...'

Emily knew she had no real reason to believe him and yet - the way he spoke - he sounded so sincere.

'We're working on it but, for now... Just record whatever. Look like you're playing by their rules and you're grateful for the tablet...'

The door suddenly opened, revealing another guard. He'd been sent in to make sure everything was above board given that those watching felt like it was all taking too long. 'Everything okay?'

Lucas lied, 'She's just struggling to think of what to say.'

The other guard was far less friendly. 'You either want to record a message, or you don't. If you can't think of anything, we'll just take it away now.'

'It's okay,' Emily said, 'I'm ready to record it.'

The guard nodded. 'Well hurry up then.' He turned to Lucas, clear distrust in his eyes, he said, 'You can wait outside. I'll take it from here.'

'It's no problem,' Lucas said.

'I said, you can wait outside.' It wasn't a request; it was an instruction. Not wanting to push his luck, Lucas stepped from the room. The guard turned his attention back to Emily. 'Hurry up.'

Part Seven
Before

Chapter Twenty-six

A large hall, tucked away down a back alley close to the centre of town. Outside, people walked by with their minds stuck on whatever was bothering them that day; what's for dinner, must pay that bill, got to pick the kids up; thoughts from the mundane to the more serious. All of those passing were entirely oblivious to the meeting taking place within the hall.

Lucas was inside, standing by a stale pot of coffee with a look of disappointment on his face. He was sick and tired of these get-togethers and not just because of the crappy coffee and piss-weak tea. Week in, week out and all they did was get together and discuss the corporation and how "evil" it was but, from where he could see it, there wasn't ever much action. They often spoke about bringing it down, along with all those working there pulling the strings, but it was just talking for the sake of it and he was sick of the inaction. He'd even told his friend, Jake Roberts, that he wouldn't be attending the meeting today. He was "out". Jake understood Lucas's frustrations but promised today would be different. He'd said to "give it one last go". Apparently today was going to change everything. All talk of course. So far the meeting was going just as it always did.

'You okay?' Jake approached from behind. He reached past Lucas and picked up the teapot before pouring himself a plastic cup of what looked like nothing more than warm milk.

'You said today was going to be different. So far… It's just the same hot air, isn't it?'

Jake smiled. 'It's all good. She's just running late.'

'She?'

Jake's smile broadened. 'I'm not supposed to say but given it's happening now, I can't see the harm.' He explained, 'We got someone.'

'You got someone?'

'Someone willing to talk.'

'Who?'

'Does it matter? All that matters is, they're going to work with us. They're going to leak information to us and help bring the whole house of cards tumbling down.'

'And you can trust them? For all we know it's a disgruntled employee with an axe to grind. They give us fake information, we leak it, we look stupid when it turns out to be bullshit. Or worse, we get sued, or end up in prison and, meanwhile, the company feels none of it.'

Jake leaned closer and whispered to stop others from hearing ahead of the great reveal, 'She's one of the doctors. And she has all the proof we need.' He took a step back. 'Also, we can use our common sense. If we think it's bullshit, we say thank you very much and continue as we were. And you, as you said, can just stop coming.' He smiled. 'But wouldn't it be great if it's *not* bullshit. That this was what we've been waiting for all this time? That we can finally bring them down and reveal exactly what goes on there… Prove that all the rumours of animal testing and such is real?' That's as far as the group thought it went at the moment: Animal testing in cruel, cramped conditions and unnecessary abuse. Their conversations were always about getting inside pictures of the animals being experimented on to leak out to the press and once the members of public got to see them, there'd be protests and it would all get shut down.

The door opened and Dr. Jackie Schwartz stepped into the hall. All eyes turned to her. Unsure she was in the right place, she said, 'You're expecting me, I believe?'

A grey-haired man in his sixties jumped up from his seat and approached their guest with an extended hand. 'Jackie?'

'That's right.'

'Glynn. Thank you for coming.'

As Glynn made the introductions, Jake turned to Lucas and said, 'This is what we've been hoping for but if you want to leave now, that's on you. No one will stop you. But it would be a shame not to hear what she had to say after all this time, wouldn't it?' He had a point.

Glynn called out, 'Okay if everyone would like to take their seat.' The seats, uncomfortable plastic chairs with rigid backs, had been set up in a circle formation in the centre of the room. Glynn was standing next to his own chair with Dr. Schwartz standing to his side. He waited for the group, men and women of mixed ages and from different backgrounds, to sit. When everyone was as comfortable as the plastic chairs allowed, he continued, 'I would like to introduce you to Jackie, one of the doctors working within the corporation.' His informal introduction was at Jackie's request. Given she'd signed NDAs ahead of accepting the job there, she didn't think it would be sensible to give a room full of strangers her full details. If just one of them was a rat, planted by the very company she worked for, her contract would be terminated, and she stood the chance of being heavily sued. He turned to Jackie and said, 'No point having me waffle on… If you'd like to introduce yourself, you can probably do it better than me.' He sat. Jackie remained standing.

Jackie looked to the different faces. All eyes were on her. 'As your colleague said, I'm one of the doctors. I haven't been with them very long and, truth be told, didn't really know what I was getting involved with when I took the job. Had I known, I would have run but… I'm there now so figured it would be better to stay and start building a case against them.' She continued, 'We've seen you protesting outside the gates before now; wanting an end to animal cruelty but, let me tell you, there is *no* animal cruelty taking place…'

Jake snorted. 'Well, that's bullshit.' The disappointment was obvious on his face. He thought she was going to blow the whistle on everything that was happening but, straight away, it sounded like she was about to try and defend the business. Next she'd probably be saying how all the workers there are good, kind, compassionate people. Lucas gave him a look; *You kept me here for this?*

'They don't test on animals because,' she continued, 'they test on *people*. Kind of.'

Glynn frowned. 'Kind of? Well, they either do or they don't.'

Jackie continued, 'I'm not sure if they started with animals but they have found a way to clone people. Each person cloned is put in a room and monitored to see how they react to the cloning process. So far most only survive a few days before going into a seizure. When this happens, the experiment is terminated before they make tweaks to the process and try again.' She added, 'The first time I saw it happen, I tried to help the patient only for one of the guards to come in and put a bullet in them. I've seen it firsthand.'

A voice from the group said, 'That's awful.'

Another voice asked, 'Who are they cloning?'

'And why?'

Chapter Twenty-seven

Sam sat opposite her potential client, Annabelle Hawkins. Annabelle was a wealthy woman in her late fifties. Her healthy bank accounts evident from the clothes and jewellery she wore.

The pair were sitting in an office within the complex. It wasn't Sam's usual office. This one was more modest in its appearance although some of the expensive artwork Sam liked to collect hung from the walls to give the otherwise white room a sense of sophistication. There was also a large fish tank in the corner because someone somewhere had read that fish were "calming".

Annabelle had been given a tour of the facilities. Most notably she'd been shown the cooking room where two bodies were currently "baking" on the tables, ready for another test run in the cloning procedure.

'Now obviously none of this has been cheap,' Sam said, 'but we are close now. With each test we do we are learning, adapting and edging closer and closer to the perfect clone.' She leaned back in her chair and continued, 'Imagine it. You get to go and enjoy life, an early retirement. Your clone continues working on your behalf while you emigrate to warmer climates and spend the rest of your days soaking up the sun on a beach someplace hot.'

'I don't think I understand how this is supposed to work. The clone has my memories? Why would they be happy to continue doing all the work while I'm away taking in the rays?'

'They will have your core memories, yes. But tweaking the mind is actually the easiest part of everything we've done. We will ensure that, when the clones are ready to be deployed, they will have no recollection of where they've come from. For all intents and purposes, they'll be *you* and getting on with *your* life, but you'll be reaping the rewards.'

'So, there'll be two of us.'

'That's right.'

'But one income.'

Sam smiled. 'This is only available to those who have *enough* of an income where it could *easily* stretch to provide comfortable lives for two.'

'But won't they notice their money is going from the bank?'

'That's down to you how you wish to make that work,' Sam said. 'We've had other clients set up fake charitable foundations as a tax avoidance scheme. We've also had others put themselves on the pay-roll under a fake name and title… There's ways of doing it but that's really down to you.' Sam shrugged. 'We've even had clients ask us *not* to wipe the memories of the clones. Their plan being to spread the time evenly. They get a couple of years relaxing while the other person works. They then swap positions… How it works is entirely down to what *you* are looking for. We're just here offering the chance to make things easier for yourself.'

'I'm almost scared to ask but what's the cost?'

'As an early investor we're offering you the chance to get it at a slightly discounted rate but I'm sure you can appreciate the science behind this isn't exactly cheap.' Sam reached into her pocket and withdrew a folded piece of paper. She handed it to Annabelle who opened it. Her eyes widened. 'I guess it all depends what price you put on your own happiness,' Sam continued. 'We work hard to get where we are in life. It's a shame we rarely take the foot off the gas and *enjoy* all we've achieved.'

'And if I wanted to go ahead with this, what would you need from me?'

'The most important thing we ask is for your discretion. Obviously we would like to keep this under wraps as, I'm sure you can appreciate, it's not exactly *approved* by the government at this stage. What we're doing here would raise a lot of eyebrows, especially from those who couldn't afford the services for themselves. You know how it is with such people; if they can't have something, they like to try and make it so others can't either.' She continued, 'We would also ask for a deposit which would help us reach the finishing line. At the moment, every pound raised is going into the program to ensure the best results for everyone and as already mentioned, this doesn't come cheap.'

'No. I can see that.' She frowned. 'But what's to stop the clones from telling people what they are.'

'It would be a hell of a story. I'm sure most people would just think the person was spinning them a tale, but the clones would also be subject to the same contracts you sign, including the NDA you signed before this meeting,' Sam said. She cut to the chase, 'So how do you feel about this?'

Annabelle smiled. 'More free time would be nice. I guess my question would be: What happens if this *did* get out?'

Chapter Twenty-eight

'Fines. Possibly prison sentence for those involved, maybe even going all the way down to the staff employed to work there. I don't know what happens when this becomes public knowledge, but it needs to stop and, if you're willing to get the information out there, I'm happy to feed you the information on whatever I can sneak out,' Jackie said, continuing addressing the group as they took in everything she had to say. 'But it's not just a question of what happens to those who work within the company but, also, what happens to the experiments. The test subjects are clones of dead people so what happens if the government does step in? What legal rights would a clone have? Or, because the person they're cloned from is deceased, would they be terminated because they shouldn't be here?' She added, 'Once the truth does come out it will open a whole new can of worms and problems that we've not seen before.'

'And what does that look like?' Glynn asked.

Jackie shrugged. 'I have no idea. Maybe the government bodies will just try and brush it all under the carpet.'

Lucas wasn't buying it. 'How do we know you're not just some disgruntled employee looking to cause trouble for them? Like, clones? This sounds like something out of a science-fiction story.'

'Yes it does, doesn't it.' Jackie wasn't about to pretend it didn't sound far-fetched. If she were sitting in their position now, she wouldn't have believed it either. 'But I'll get you the proof you require. I'm not sure how yet, obviously I need to be careful…'

Lucas continued, 'And you still *chose* to work there.'

'I didn't know what they were involved in to begin with.'

'You could have left when you realised.'

'I could have, yes. But what good would that have done? The experiments would continue, people on the outside would still believe they were "just" testing on animals… Or I could stay there as long as I can and try and gather all the information so someone such as you, or your friends, could expose them for who they really are and what they're really doing.' She admitted, 'After trying to help the patient when they had a seizure, I was pulled to one side and berated by management so, for all I know, I'm about to be fired anyway. I know they want to have another meeting with me. And, if that does happen, then unfortunately there's not much else I can do but… We'll cross that bridge when we get to it.' She looked around the room. Everyone was watching her in a state of disbelief. Such were their expressions; she wasn't entirely sure how much of this they were even hearing anymore. Or whether they were believing anything she had said. She checked her watch. 'Well, I have a shift soon so need to make a move. Are you interested in what I have to say, or should we call it a day there?'

Glynn shook his head. 'No. We're interested. But we're going to need proof. No disrespect.'

'None taken. I didn't expect you to automatically believe everything I had to say. As you pointed out, it's all straight from the realms of science-fiction. Even if you did believe me, it's fair to say others would require proof anyway. If you're interested in helping me get the story out there though, I'm happy to try and get you what you need.'

Glynn said, 'Well you have my number.'

'And you have mine but, for security, I would appreciate it if you didn't use it unless it's an emergency. I'm sure you can understand I'm going to need to be extremely careful. I've already seen how they handle accidents in the work place and I'd rather not be a statistic for another one of the buried files,' she said, referring to what had happened to Dr. Chappo. At this stage, all she really knew about Chappo's death was that it had been a workplace accident. Hardly anyone knew of the truth although, when Jackie had her meeting the following week, offering her another placement within the company, that was one mystery which would be cleared up. For now, she just knew that he'd died and his family had been heavily compensated.

'So, it sounds like we're in agreement,' Glynn said.

Jackie smiled. She hadn't been sure what to expect when she agreed to meet with the group. Having seen them outside the complex before, she wasn't sure whether they would have really been interested in exposing the truth or whether they were simply content with making a nuisance of themselves, waving their little signs around. 'Good. Well, you'll have to forgive me, but I'll be on my way then. They really don't like it when you're late.'

Chapter Twenty-nine

A few weeks had passed since Dr. Schwartz had approached the group. Without hearing from her since, the meetings had gone back to "all talk and no action". They'd even stopped doing the protesting given what Jackie had said about the lack of animal testing happening within the complex. Why protest something that wasn't *actually* happening?

Having grown tired of the inaction, Lucas had stopped going to the meetings. They felt like a waste of time given the lack of progress in moving forward and he felt his time was better served elsewhere. Most notably the bottom of a whiskey bottle.

Lucas lived alone in a quiet apartment block in the city. High rates, higher rent and with the cost of food shopping practically doubling over the last few months, it didn't leave much spare income to go out and "enjoy" himself. It didn't help that he was in-between jobs at the moment; one downside to leaving college with no clear goal as to what he wanted to do being that he found himself going from job to job. In the "in-between" moments, the benefits he received barely covered the bills, let alone left much to spend elsewhere. Especially after he'd bought his alcohol; his best friend at the moment while he continued slipping into a deeper depression, no doubt not helped by the lack of social interaction he had now.

Just as he took the last mouthful from the bottle in hand, there was a knock on the front door of the apartment. He frowned. He couldn't recall the last time he'd had someone come and visit - at least not without being invited and he'd certainly not invited anyone.

He pulled himself out of his armchair and made his way to the front door. He pulled it open to reveal Jake standing there with a beaming smile on his face. 'I have the answer to your job problems,' he said as he waved a newspaper in the air. He noticed the empty bottle in Lucas's hand. 'Presuming you haven't found anything yet.' Without waiting to be invited, Jake stepped into the apartment. He slapped the newspaper against Lucas's chest and held it there until Lucas took it for himself. 'I circled it for you.'

Sensing this wasn't a fleeting visit, Lucas closed the front door before glancing down at the paper. Sure enough, Jake had circled one of the many job listings. 'Security guard?'

'You have the experience, don't you?'

'Well yes…'

'Look who it's for.'

Lucas scanned the advert. 'Oh shit.'

'Oh, shit indeed.' The advert was for the very same corporation they wanted to expose. Dr. Schwartz had stopped talking to them and clearly wasn't coming back with any additional information for them but a job as a security guard? If Lucas was successful, he'd have access to all areas. 'Can you imagine the information you'd have access to? All the shit you could learn from working there? If ever we had an opportunity to see what is going on behind those gates, this is it and… Well… You're the one with the experience to get the job.' He glanced at the bottle. 'If you can stop drinking long enough to breeze the interview process, that is.'

Lucas frowned. 'I'm not an alcoholic. It's not like I'm drinking every day.' He set the bottle to the side hoping the conversation would end there. 'You really think the security guards see anything there though? Surely we'll be on the outside, stopping people from going through?'

'I can't see them having security who *wouldn't* have complete access to the place. They'd need to know the building inside and out in case there's ever any trouble. Even if they do put you outside the main area, they'd still give you a guided tour so you can get your bearings and learn where everything is. I'm telling you; this is a *great* opportunity for us. For the group. And worst case scenario, it's a job for you.'

Having not had much luck on the job front recently, that was a valid point to consider. Any job was better than no job, even if it was working for the "enemy."

'What do you think? You going to apply for it?' If only to add further encouragement, Jake said, 'One of us needs to and, out of everyone in the group, you're the one with the experience…' Not to be a dick but to speak the truth, he added, 'You're also the one who needs the work…' A fair comment given that the others either had jobs, weren't in a position to work or were retired. He said again, 'I think this is a great opportunity for us.'

On paper it did sound like a good opportunity for sure, but one thing bothered Lucas. He asked, 'What happened to the woman who was working there? Has anyone heard from her or was there another "accident" in the work place, like the last guy she told us about?'

Jake shrugged. 'She said she had another meeting with them after she made that mistake… Maybe they let her go?'

'Did Glynn even try reaching out to her? What if they caught her trying to smuggle information out and the punishment was more *severe* than she imagined?' While it might have seemed farfetched for a company to bump off the staff who were threatening to ruin their reputation, it wasn't entirely out of the realms of possibilities. One example: How many politicians had died in strange circumstances?

'Truthfully? I don't know if Glynn reached out to her. I can ask him.'

'I just think I would be more comfortable applying for a job if I knew she was alive… She mentioned that guy who had an accident in the workplace, she said about the test subject who had a bullet put through their brains… It doesn't sound like these people mess around. Me taking a job there? Sounds like I'm the one taking all the risks.'

Jake didn't have an answer for him. In his head the scenario painted seemed somewhat unlikely but there was certainly no denying that it *was* Lucas who'd be taking all the risks. Even if they did "just" dismiss him, there was still a chance they could try to sue him and if they did? It was fair to say the rest of the group wouldn't step forward to help pay any court costs. After a pause, Jake shrugged. 'I mean, it was worth showing you. If it's not of interest or you think it's a bad idea - just forget it.' He smiled. 'Pretend I never said anything.'

He went to take the paper away, but Lucas pulled it from his reach. 'I never said *no* just… I had questions.' He added, 'I'll think about it.' Take away the fact the company was, apparently, a shit-house - it was still a job and, right now, any job was better than no job.

Jake could see the thought process running through Lucas's mind and quickly backtracked, 'Well if you do end up going for it… That's entirely up to you. Not like I have a gun to your head, and you do raise some valid concerns. In the meantime, I'll ask Glynn if he did reach out to the doctor. Maybe he did and she said she couldn't help us anymore. Maybe he was too embarrassed to tell us, after we all got our hopes up that, finally, we were moving in the right direction.'

'Well, let me know what he says. In the meantime, I'll have a think…'

Jake nodded towards the empty bottle of whiskey and said, 'Maybe without the added *help* of the booze in your system?'

Lucas sighed. 'I'm not drunk; I'm relaxed.'

Chapter Thirty

Dr. Schwartz apologised, 'I'm sorry. I can't help you. I no longer work in that department anymore. They moved me elsewhere.' She was on the phone to Glynn.

Despite being told to contact her in case of emergencies only, he *had* to reach out given Lucas was considering the advertised job. While he was disappointed to hear she wasn't able to help them anymore, Glynn was at least thankful to hear that she wasn't dead or sacked. 'I understand,' Glynn said, unable to hide the disappointment in his tone. 'It's a shame but I get it.'

Jackie didn't bother telling Glynn about the new experiment she'd been put in charge of. It would have certainly raised eyebrows from people outside in the real world and caused the corporation *a lot* of problems if it were ever leaked, but it was a job and a chance for her to prove herself and, all being good, progress further up the career ladder. Just as they were for everyone else, times were hard and the last thing she wanted to do was lose a job and find herself back on the breadline again. It had been hard enough to find *this* job, let alone have the whole department closed down only for the staff to find themselves in direct competition in searching for work elsewhere. Never before had there been a more apt saying: Do not bite the hand that feeds you. Currently, this hand was most definitely "feeding her".

It was only after she hung the call up that she realised she should have said she'd been lying anyway. A chance to throw them off the scent and stop pestering the company. But then, maybe that would have sounded more suspicious? In some cases, it was always better to give minimal information. This was one of those cases.

Glynn had made the call in front of both Jake and Lucas. He put his phone back in his pocket and said, 'She's alive at least. Not sure if you heard her but they moved her to a new department so - she's not going to be able to get us the proof she promised.'

'A shame,' Jake said.

Glynn nodded. 'But she *is* alive so…' He turned his attention to Lucas. 'I'm sure Jake already told you when he saw the job advert but if ever there was an opportunity to see things from the inside… This is it. This is our chance.'

'And if they don't have me stationed anywhere with anything untoward?'

'You have a decent paying job with good benefits,' Glynn said. 'I think, for you, the best case would be that you *can't* find anything bad there because at least you know you'll be settled in a "good" company. And if there are things there that need to be shown to the rest of the world? Well…'

'I have a choice between keeping quiet, earning decent money or getting myself sacked because the company's closed down after I expose them,' Lucas said. He couldn't help but wonder how it would play out if he saw anything bad there. On the one hand, he hated the idea of the animal testing they believed was happening. He'd like nothing more than to close all that down. On the other hand, though, it would be paying his bills and - there were *always* bills which needed to be paid.

'I guess that comes down to your conscience,' Glynn said. 'If you're happy working in such an environment then… I guess you tell us there's nothing to be seen there and we move on, taking you at your word. But I think I know you… I don't think you'd stay quiet if you saw anything.'

With his debt continually mounting, Lucas couldn't say for sure. The benefits barely covered the bills. Could he be happy working in a place where they tested on animals or humans? It wasn't like it would be *him* who'd be running the experiments. Or would it eat at him until he shouted it from the rooftops? In this present moment, he had no idea what kind of person he'd be in that situation. 'Well, I guess... First things first I need to get the job before I stress about things like that.'

Glynn laughed. 'Imagine all this and you *don't* get it.'

'Times are hard out there. A lot of unemployed people,' Lucas had already started to make his excuses on the off-chance he failed to get the job.

'Best wear your best suit then.'

Jake laughed. 'Not sure about that. Can you polish a turd?'

Neither Lucas nor Glynn saw the funny side.

Part Eight
Today

Chapter Thirty-one

Lucas's words kept playing through in Emily's head as she sat alone in the white room: *The real you died in a car crash on the way to get your daughter from school.* As she sat there, her mind racing at a million miles per hour, she was frantically trying to remember anything about *that* day; when she first woke and found herself in the other room with the stranger, James. She remembered the traffic jam, she recalled turning off the main route to find another way and then - nothing.

With no clock in the room, she had no idea how long it had been since she'd been given the opportunity to film a video for her daughter. Her video was short and succinct; shorter than she would have liked but it was off-putting having the guard watching over her, a stern look on his impatient face. She told her daughter she loved her; she said that she was okay and - the news her daughter would have wanted to hear - she'd be home soon. She finished the video saying how much she loved her, forcing a smile to keep up the pretence that she was "happy" and "well". There was more she could have said but she knew, if she went on too long, there'd definitely be no chance of getting them to send it on. Although with what the other guard had told her, she was doubting it would be going anywhere anyway. Still, she couldn't lose the little hope she had.

As for his words: Could there have been any truth in what he'd said? Had she been involved in an accident that took her life and had *these people* managed to clone her and bring her back? It all sounded so far-fetched but, in a way, it made *sense* and that's what frightened her the most.

Her racing mind was momentarily distracted when the overhead light clicked from white to red, signalling that someone was coming in. Well-conditioned for this moment, she moved to the corner of the room. A moment later, the door opened and the familiar sound of the trolley's wheels squeaked into the room.

'How are you liking the private room?'

Emily recognised the voice although she didn't know Tammie's name. It was the same nurse who'd been seeing her while she was locked in the other room. Unsure what else to say and not willing to reveal she knew the truth, she said, 'It's nice. I prefer it.'

'That's good then. We weren't sure if people would get lonely when in a room by themselves but with the way your last room-mate was going, we presumed you would prefer this.'

'Definitely.'

'Anyway, I'm just here to take your blood pressure and temperature.'

'Okay.' Emily didn't bother looking back; she held her arm out to make it easier for Tammie. Tammie applied the sleeve and took Emily's blood pressure. When she was done, she removed the sleeve.

'The guard that brought you in here… They've asked me to find out if he said anything to you.'

Emily frowned. 'Said anything?'

'Okay. Your temperature.' She handed Emily the thermometer which she duly put under her tongue. 'Like, if he tried talking to you?' She paused a moment before taking the thermometer back again. 'Okay that's all good too.'

If he'd spoken the truth, *that guard* was the closest thing Emily had to an ally in here and she wasn't about to throw him under the bus. 'He said I could record a video message.'

'That was it?'

'I didn't know what to say so he just told me to speak from the heart,' she lied; the best acting she'd done since being on stage for a college production. College. She had all of her memories, other than how she got into the initial white room. If she were a clone, would the memories have also come across or was this proof enough that she was her normal self and the guard was just messing with her? If he *was* messing with her then - mission accomplished; her brain was scrambled. Keen to avoid further questions, she decided to throw them back to the nurse instead. 'How come?'

'I probably shouldn't say anything, but we've been having problems with him. He aced all the tests to get the job but… Let's just say he has quite the active imagination. Honestly, some of the stories he's come out with in the staff room… Probably should have been a screenwriter, or something.' She changed the subject as she picked up the menu for the next day's meals, 'This is for you.'

Emily took the menu. Same as before; a list of meals not normally associated with hospital food. 'Thank you.'

'Just call your menu through. They'll be listening.'

'Do you know if they watched my video? For my daughter, that is? Did they watch it? Was it okay? Are they going to send it?'

'I'm sorry but that's not something I'm privy too. But I'm sure they'll send it after asking you to record it.'

'Okay.' The nurse's words brought Emily no peace of mind.

'And I'll see you tomorrow,' Tammie said. She pushed the trolley towards the door. When close enough, it opened from the other side. Without a further word, she stepped from the room and the door closed again. The light turned from red to white and - she was alone again. Her noisy mind flicked to thoughts of James and what was happening in *his* room now they'd been separated. A burning question: Was he being "punished" as per their promise to those who disobeyed them when they first awoke to find themselves in the room…?

Chapter Thirty-two

James watched the laptop screen intently, unsure of what he was being shown and the reasons as to why; video footage of these white-jellied *things* growing on a table beneath heat lamps normally seen in vivariums. Kiefel had just walked straight into the room with a laptop, thrust it at him and told him to watch the assortment of video clips she'd moved to her otherwise empty desktop. 'What the fuck is this supposed to be?' He frowned when the camera turned to the last table in the room. He was lying on it in a pool of white liquid. The clip stopped there.

He looked up to Kiefel and shrugged, hoping she was about to answer his abrupt question. She did, but not with an answer. 'Click the next video,' she said.

James hesitated. 'Or you could just tell me what the fuck I am meant to be watching.' The guard, standing next to Kiefel with his rifle aimed directly at James, stepped one step closer to James with his finger ready on the trigger. James got the message and clicked the second video in the series of films lined up for him.

The film loaded. The White Room came onto the screen. James was on one bed, Emily on thc other. She was awake but he was still sleeping, obvious confusion and fear on her face as she looked around trying to make sense of where she was and how she got there. 'That's not right,' James said. 'I woke up before her.'

'This time round,' Kiefel said. She leaned to the computer and fast forwarded the clip until the end.

On screen: James and Emily were standing, surrounded by the debris of broken plates on the floor. James's hand was bleeding with white blood. He raised his hand towards the mirror, showing the self-inflicted damage and yelled, 'What the fuck is this shit?'

A voice boomed through the computer's adequate speakers, 'Please move to your corners of the room. *Now.*'

'Fuck this. Tell us what the fuck is going on!' Mocking the mystery person's voice, James sarcastically added, '*Now.*'

Watching the footage, confused about what he was looking at, James asked, 'So what is this? One of those Deep Fake videos? An A.I thing?'

In the film, the door opened and two armed guards stormed into the room. In perfect unison they both raised their guns, each one choosing which of the two to put down. No words. No warnings. They squeezed their triggers and dropped both James and Emily in an instant. The video automatically looped back to the start before Kiefel stopped it.

'You've been in the room before,' Kiefel said. 'As you can see, it didn't have the best of endings and I'm sure you can appreciate this one is heading in the same direction, which is why I took it upon myself to try something new with you.'

'Something new? Been here before? What are you even fucking talking about?'

Kiefel selected the next clip and hit the space bar. The video started to play. The footage was taken from the cooking room again; time lapse footage showing a white puddle slowly form into a human shape until it was left with James laying there once again with tubes sticking from various parts of his body. When the tubes were removed, one of the "cooks" smeared a white gel over the wound-site and, again through time lapse footage, it healed over leaving no signs of anything ever being there. Kiefel explained, 'You are a clone of yourself. You, the *real* you, had a heart attack at work. We have a deal in place where we get to go in and take DNA samples of the recently deceased. From those samples we then grow replicas. You, sitting here now, are a replica of the man you once were. Perfect in almost every sense apart from your blood.'

James started to laugh. 'Okay whatever drugs you are on, I would like some too please. Sounds like a hell of a ride.'

Kiefel turned to the guard and gave a nod of her head. He lowered his rifle, tucking it behind his back and leaving it dangling on the shoulder strap before. Without any words, he pulled a blade from a utility belt around his waist. In a quick motion he stepped forward, grabbed James's hand and ran the blade across James's open palm. James let out a cry of pain as he pulled his hand back against his chest. 'What the fuck are you doing?'

'Look at the wound,' Kiefel said.

'You're fucking insane.' James looked at his hand and was stunned into silence by the sight of white blood oozing from the wound.

'You and your ex-room-mate, Emily, have survived the longest on this go around,' Kiefel said. 'We believe we're almost at the end of the experiment. Almost in a position to offer rich people the ability to clone themselves so they can get the clone to continue working for them while they go and enjoy what time they have left on this planet. An easy ticket to early retirement.' Kiefel said, 'Your behaviour cannot and will not be tolerated. At the moment we have a choice, tell you the truth or terminate you and start the whole process again hoping that the third time, will see a different outcome. Needless to say, so close to the end, we're not wanting to start the process from scratch. We would rather try and salvage what we have, which is why we moved Emily to a room of her own.'

'This is insane...'

'You are a clone, James. The real you is dead. You will not be returning to the life you once had but we can ensure you live a good, happy life here with us - giving you everything you want or… We can start again with a new version of you.' She looked at his hand. 'Obviously if you wish to proceed with us, we will get your room cleaned up and make you more comfortable here. We will also get your wound tended to by one of our nurses here. The choice is entirely up to you and all dependent on whether you can play nice.'

James said nothing. He was looking at his hand. The look on his face showed he was trying hard to process all that he'd been told.

Kiefel knew it would have been a lot to take in though and, if necessary, was prepared to give him the time to make sense of it all and decide what he wanted to do. 'Would you like some time to think things through?'

James, still stunned into silence, nodded.

'Very well. When you're ready to talk, you can call for me through the mirror and someone will come and get me. My name is Dr. Kiefel.' She didn't bother to check whether he'd taken any of that in. She turned and left the room. The guard hung back until Kiefel was in the clear and - then - followed, closing the door behind him.

James raised his hand to his mouth and tentatively licked the wound. He flinched at the taste; more chemical-based than the coppery flavouring blood usually had.

Chapter Thirty-three

Dr. Howard practically pounced on Kiefel the moment she walked back round to the viewing room. Unsure whether Kiefel was doing the right thing, Chmielewski had decided to go and have a meeting of her own to highlight what was happening. In fairness, Kiefel had half-expected her to anyway. Whenever there were changes within the company, it seemed to bring out the worst in the staff as they all stepped up their game in an extra effort to ensure their own role was safe. Because Kiefel had been expecting Dr. Chmielewski to "snitch" on her, she was ready with an excuse when Dr. Howard asked, 'What the hell do you think you're doing?'

'You were in a meeting. We had a problem. I had to make an executive decision on how to handle it and this is the path I chose.'

Dr. Howard had watched the whole back and forth between Kiefel and James. 'And what if he decides you're lying in an effort to try and regain some control? What if he decides to push back?'

Kiefel smiled. 'He was already pushing back. How do you think that shit stain got on the mirror? Do you think we went in there and put it there ourselves? The way I saw it, I had two options. The first option was to put a bullet in him and start the test from the beginning. The second choice, the one I went for, was to tell him the truth. If he pushes back, he gets a bullet. And he's alone, it's not like he can tell anyone about what's going on, is it?' Kiefel was also quick to point out, 'We've also moved the other patient to her own room... She keeps asking to record a video message to send to her daughter to stop her from worrying so, I'd even arranged for her to record that. And no, before you ask, we will obviously not be sending the file on. But she doesn't know that and thinks we've done something good for her which, in turn, helps keep her in line for the time-being too.' On the off chance there was any misunderstanding, Kiefel said, 'Everything is under control, just as it was before Sam decided to bring you on board.'

'If that were true, Sam *wouldn't* have brought me in,' Howard snapped straight back. 'Also, I hear that there's a chance one of the guards could have been having a private conversation with the other patient too? When he was waiting for her to make her little home-video… That he had his back to the mirror and was saying something quietly that we couldn't make out?'

'That's how it looked, yes, and - again - I took control of that too. Tammie, one of her longest-standing nurses, was sent in earlier than scheduled to take the vitals. While doing so, we had her ask the patient to see if he'd said anything to her. Apparently they talked about her not knowing what to say in the video. Nothing she said to Tammie suggested anything different.'

'Either way I'll be pulling *him* to one side so I can question him directly,' Dr. Howard said. So that there were no further misunderstandings, she made it clear, 'Whatever happens in these experiments; everything needs to come through me. Understood?'

Kiefel smiled sweetly but beneath said smile there was nothing but contempt. 'Of course.' As if to prove she was nothing but a team player, she continued, 'I'm very sorry if my actions have upset you. I knew you were busy, so I took control of the situation.'

Howard ignored the apology and said again, 'Like I said, everything *must* come through me first. If a decision needs to be made, I'll make it.'

'Understood.'

Without having anything else to say to Dr. Kiefel, Howard walked from the room. Kiefel turned towards Chmielewski and glared at her with a self-satisfied grin. In her head, she was simply thinking, *Fuck you*. Chmielewski, in turn, turned away as her face began to flush from embarrassment. Not wanting to let the moment slide, and not wanting there to be *any* doubt Kiefel knew it had been Chmielewski who'd run off to Dr. Howard, she said, 'And next time you're not happy about something I am doing, perhaps try having a conversation with me first? I don't recall you protesting much when I said what I was going to do.'

Chmielewski said nothing. The one guard in the room also stayed quiet, choosing - instead - to keep his head down so as not to get dragged into the middle of anything. He was there, being paid, to watch the subject and *not* get involved with internal politics and, as he saw it, general bullshit.

Chapter Thirty-four

After being removed from Emily's new room, Lucas had been sent on his break; a chance for management to talk to Emily to see if he'd said anything to her that he shouldn't have, not that they told him that's what they were planning.

There was a part of Lucas that wanted to just grab his personal belongings and get the hell out of there as he'd known he'd crossed a line he shouldn't have, but another part, the larger of the two, wanted to stay because he knew he'd not got the necessary proof to take to the group. At the moment, all he had was his word of what he'd seen and - that wouldn't hold up. Not if they truly wanted to make a difference.

When he walked into the cafeteria, his heart was still racing from the adrenaline that first surged when he'd decided to tell Emily the truth. He could feel the blood pumping around his body, making him feel both hot and uncomfortable although he tried his best to hide it from others already on their break; not that anyone really noticed him. In a company this large, making friends wasn't easy given it was a different face on every shift. It was harder for the guards to make acquaintances given, even if they did work the same shift pattern as others, they were always working alone, guarding whatever door they were put on. And speaking of doors, Lucas already had a feeling he'd be moved to a spot on the far side of the complex now, away from the experiments.

After pouring himself a cup of coffee, marginally better than the coffee on offer in the meetings he used to attend, he went and sat in one of the far corners away from the others. As was often the way, since working in security, he positioned himself with his back to the wall and facing the door so he could watch who came and went. It was an old technique he'd been taught by someone with military training that had just stuck with him because *it just made sense.* More so given he was, technically, sitting in "enemy territory".

As he sat there nursing his hot drink, he watched staff come and go. None of them even so much as glanced in his direction; each too busy to make the most of their own break by grabbing food from the vending machine, a hot drink from the pot and sitting down with their tablet or book. One woman even sat in the adjacent corner and put her head down on the table in front of her, keen to close her eyes if only for fifteen minutes. Clearly it had been a long shift. It was also evident that this woman didn't work in the same department he'd been stationed in because if she knew what was going on behind *those* closed doors, she most likely wouldn't have been comfortable closing her eyes around such people.

Just as Lucas's heart-rate was getting back down to a more "normal" pattern, the door opened and Dr. Jackie Schwartz walked in. She stopped in her tracks when she saw Lucas sitting in the corner. His heart skipped a beat. With a quick glance around the room, she made her way across to where he was sitting and took a chair opposite. 'I didn't know you *worked* here,' she said.

'New starter. Not sure it's for me.'

'A guard I see.'

'Yep. Got to pay the bills.'

'Uh huh.'

To anyone listening, the conversation was about as mundane as it could get. To both Dr. Schwartz and Lucas though, it was more about what *wasn't* being said.

'So how are you finding it?'

Lucas smiled. 'Interesting, I guess you could say.'

The door opened behind her and Sam walked in. A woman with a purpose, with the way she automatically came over to Lucas, it was as though she already knew where he was before she'd even set foot into the room. 'Lucas. May I borrow you for a minute?' Her voice startled Jackie; with her back to the door, she'd not noticed Sam enter the room.

'What can I do for you?'

Trying to remain composed, Dr. Schwartz turned to face Sam as she asked, 'Did you want me to leave?'

'No, you're good.' Sam pulled another chair up to join them at the table. Jackie could feel her face flush, a look of guilt in her eyes. She was thankful Sam didn't seem to be paying her any attention. She also noticed how calm Lucas appeared to be despite having Sam's undivided attention solely on him. 'I hear you gave one of the patients a tablet so they could record a message?'

'That's what I was told to do, yes.'

'And did you say anything to her?'

'We spoke, yes.'

Sam smiled, thankful that he didn't try and lie. 'May I ask what you spoke about?'

'She said she wasn't sure what to say. She'd been asking to record the message for a while now but hadn't stopped to consider what she was going to say.'

'I see.'

Despite the fact Lucas and Emily hadn't agreed on what they'd say if they were questioned about their time together, they'd both pretty much said the same thing which helped add weight to their story. Lucas continued, 'I just told her to say whatever came to her head.'

'Is there a reason you chose to speak so softly and turn your back to the viewing window?'

Lucas frowned. 'I didn't realise that was a problem? I was just trying to offer her some reassurance. I didn't think I was doing anything wrong.'

'We don't encourage conversation with the patients.'

'Oh. Sorry. I didn't know.'

Sam smiled again. *The smile of a predator*. 'You do now.'

'I *do* now.'

'Did she say anything else to you?'

Lucas shook his head. 'Not that I can recall?' Sticking to the truth he added, 'Another guard came in and dismissed me, so I left. Then I was sent on my break.' Cutting straight to the chase, he said, 'I'm sorry, I didn't realise I was doing anything I shouldn't have. I was told to give her the tablet so she could record something for her daughter, she didn't know what to say… There really wasn't much else to it than that.'

'Well for future reference, again, we'd sooner you didn't engage in conversation with them. If they have any questions, you can pass them onto someone who's *trained* in that area.'

'Okay. Not a problem.' Unsure whether this was the end of it, Lucas went on to ask, 'Is that everything?'

'For now.' Sam got up and, without so much as a sideways glance at Dr. Schwartz, left the room.

Jackie eyed Lucas up suspiciously. '*Was* that everything?'

Lucas smiled. He wasn't about to tell her anything. Clearly, given that she'd disappeared from the meetings, she'd picked a side, and it wasn't his. He downed his coffee, almost burning his tongue in the process, before he stood and said, 'Breaks sure do go fast around here, don't they?' Before she could say anything, he promptly left.

Chapter Thirty-five

It was a new day. The rain outside was beating down, God seemingly punishing the cruel world by trying to drown everyone so He could start again for a second time; at least that's how it felt to the religious folk. For everyone else is was nothing more than a harsh end to what had already been a wash-out of a summer.

Inside the complex, people continued about their day doing whatever task they'd been assigned to. For Lucas that meant standing outside the door to Emily's room with strict instruction he wouldn't be going in unless given notice to do so. Further instruction making sure he understood that under no circumstances was he to talk to her.

Standing there, with time ticking by slowly, he couldn't help but wonder whether she'd taken onboard anything he'd said. He guessed not given there'd been no kickback from her since learning the truth. They'd continued going in to monitor her stats and taking her meals in and, according to the reports, on no occasion had she said anything or tried to escape. She was, as ever, the dutiful little test subject.

Lucas had felt sick since learning what the company was doing to these people. There was an argument to be made that they weren't really *people* anymore. The people they were moulded from were deceased, their life over. These, dwelling within the white rooms, were nothing more but a warped experiment for the rich to benefit from whenever it was ready to be revealed. Lucas had already heard through the grapevine that there was quite the waiting list of those waiting to procure such services. It was depressing how readily people were able to suck in something as *ugly* as this but, then, he wasn't exactly surprised. The obscenely rich didn't seem to have the same morals as those who were closer to the breadline.

While standing there, Lucas was trying to figure out how to get the proof he needed to take all this to the outside world. Ahead of their shifts, staff had to put their mobile phones in lockers, and a row of metal detectors were used to ensure nothing was snuck in that was forbidden. No phones, no cameras, no recording devices - even packed lunches were thoroughly scrutinised by those working the staff entrance. And if a person *was* caught with something they shouldn't have? It was a case of instant dismissal.

What made it worse was that he felt as though he couldn't turn around and leave either. How could he walk away knowing what was happening here? Whether the clones were considered to be "real people" didn't take away the fact they were being imprisoned against their will. He was stuck there until he figured a way to bring the empire crashing down and he knew his word wouldn't cut it.

Lucas glanced back towards the door and tried to imagine what she was doing on the other side of it. Was she just sitting there, on her bed, accepting her new reality or was she in there, planning a way out? All he could do was ask the nurse how she was doing the next time she came and checked on her but, even then, he knew there was little chance of the nurse stopping to pass the time with him. After yesterday, and how the staff had barely spoken to him when he arrived at work that morning, it was fair to say he'd broken what little trust he'd started building with his "colleagues".

On the other side of the room, Emily was standing by the mirror. She was just staring at her reflection, trying to see if there were any differences in her appearance between now and before she woke to find herself in the white room. One thing was for sure; she looked tired. She thought she looked a little paler too although that could have been down to the harsh light bouncing off the white walls.

Emily still didn't know what to do or what to think. Everything the guard had told her was so far-fetched that she was having trouble with processing it *and* believing it. No sane person would hear any of what he had to say and "just" go along with it. That being said, there were gaps in her memory from her last day of freedom so perhaps there could have been some truth in what had been said to her?

As she continued staring at herself, remembering the woman she once had been her eyes started to well. She frowned as a single white tear spilled over and rolled down her cheek. She wiped it away with the back of her hand and looked at the smear-mark left behind.

On the other side of the mirror Dr. Henderson was watching closely with Dr. Hall by her side. Neither of them believed the conversation between Emily and Lucas had been entirely innocent and, with Emily's actions now, it was clear she was trying to process *something*.

Dr. Hall, who'd been working the night-shift and was preparing to leave now the hand-over to Dr. Henderson had taken place, said, 'She's barely slept. I think she laid down for about ten minutes. Other than that, she's been pacing, always coming back to her reflection.' She added, 'I made a note of it in the logs.'

'So I saw.'

'Do you think he told her?'

'Honestly, I don't know. If he did, she didn't exactly react. I'm pretty sure, if I were in that position, I would have had a million and one questions and - I wouldn't have been able to *not* ask them,' Henderson said.

Hall asked, 'Think we should tell Dr. Howard?'

'She doesn't start for another couple of hours. She worked the mid-shift yesterday. I think, what I'll do, I'll send Tammie in with the breakfast. See if she says anything to her. Maybe that guard did whisper something to her and she spent the night processing it. If so, I'm sure she has questions for us this morning.'

'Did you want me to stay on for a while?'

'No. It's fine. I've got it from here. You go home and get some rest.'

'Okay, so long as you're sure.'

'I am,' Henderson said.

'If anything happens - you'll call me?'

'Sure.'

Suddenly remembering she was being monitored, in the room, Emily turned her back to the mirror. She was still staring down at the white-smear mark on the back of her hand. When she was in the other room with James, the nurse had said it was a side-effect of the medication they'd been given but - really? What if it was a side-effect of no longer being a *normal* human? An uncomfortable question popped in her head, *What exactly am I?*

Emily had been thankful when they pulled her away from the other room. With James's rising temper, she knew it wouldn't be long before he was punished and she didn't want the same treatment, guilty by association. Now, she was almost jealous of him. Or rather, jealous of the fact he didn't have the same knowledge she had. *They* say, "ignorance is bliss" and, in this case, there'd never been a truer saying.

Keeping her back to the mirror, she made her way to the bed. She sat on the corner and stared at the wall while hoping this was nothing but a nightmare. A nightmare from which she'd soon awaken.

Chapter Thirty-six

James walked over to the clean part of the mirror. After his conversation with Kiefel the previous day, it still hadn't been cleaned. Kiefel figured there was no point in doing so until he'd made his mind up on how he wanted to proceed; work with them or call it a day here and now. If he chose the latter, the room would need to be deep-cleaned ahead of the new experiment starting. If he chose to stay, they'd send in the cleaners. Giving him time to think, they'd also not bothered sending in a nurse or even providing his evening meal and drink. Why waste good food and beverage on a person who was to soon be eating a bullet? It wasn't like he'd starve to death while he made his mind up.

He knocked on the mirror and called through to those viewing, 'I'd like to speak to Dr. Kiefel.'

The voice of Chmielewski came through the speaker, 'Unfortunately Dr. Kiefel isn't in the office yet.'

James continued, 'I want to talk about what she said yesterday.' He paused, waiting for confirmation his request had been heard and would be permitted once she was in. No such confirmation came. 'Hello?' Still silence. He knocked against the mirror for a second time, harder this time around. 'Can I at least get some breakfast please? Even just some water?'

Chmielewski spoke through the intercom, 'Breakfast rounds will begin shortly.' She leaned back and de-pressed the button for the intercom's microphone. James had asked to speak to Kiefel and while she was already in the building somewhere, Chmielewski had already decided it would be a conversation she'd miss. Instead, she would wait for Dr. Howard to come in so she could take the lead after all; a move which Chmielewski knew would upset Kiefel but - there was a new pecking order now and, she needed to get used to the idea of not being in charge anymore. Chmielewski figured, if Kiefel had a problem with it, she could take it up directly with Dr. Howard. And, if she did, Chmielewski would have liked nothing more than to be a fly on the wall.

Back in the room, knowing he wasn't going to get any further with the team watching him, James turned back to the room. Looking around it, he didn't want to be stuck there indefinitely. Kiefel spoke about making him comfortable there, but they had said, right back at the start of the experiment, there'd be rewards for good behaviour but so far there'd been none. Why would she now, suddenly, start giving him a more comfortable life? Especially as, per her words, they could just pull the plug and start again with a new version of himself.

Had it not been for the footage he'd been shown, he would never have believed anything Kiefel had told him. He knew there was a chance the footage could have been made with AI but, from where he was watching, all the human models seemed to have the correct number of fingers and thumbs so… Taking it as "the truth", James knew he didn't really have many options as to where to go from here but, in the time spent alone, he thought he'd figured out a fair compromise. All he needed to do was convince Dr. Kiefel that it was the best way forward for *their* experiment.

Not wanting to wait any longer, he turned back to the mirror and knocked again. 'Can I please talk to *someone* about what I was told yesterday? I think I have a suggestion on how we could all benefit from this.' There was no response. Out of frustration, he hit the mirror with the side of his hand. He couldn't figure out why they'd bother telling him everything if they weren't then happy to hear his thoughts. He paused, taking a moment to try and calm his temper. If he wanted them to take him seriously, he knew he couldn't get angry. He needed to remain level-headed and calm. Although, if they didn't send someone in within the next few hours, he'd presume they were looking to terminate him and he'd act accordingly. As his thoughts took a darker, more aggressive turn, the lights suddenly switched from white to red.

Chmielewski's voice came through, 'Please move to the corner of the room.'

James hesitated but eventually did as he was told. The only difference was, he didn't put his back to the door this time. If they were coming in to terminate the experiment, they could look him in the eyes.

'Please turn and face the wall.'

'No,' he said.

'*Turn to face the wall.*'

'I won't. You have guns you like putting in people's faces. I'm sure you'd be able to stop me rushing whoever comes in with a simple squeeze of a trigger…' He said again, 'I won't turn around.'

There was a pause. The door opened. A tray of food, along with a boxed drink, slid in from the hallway. It made it to the middle of the room before stopping. The door slammed shut again.

James called, 'And when do I get to speak to the doctor?'

Silence.

Further down the corridor, in another room, Emily's light had also turned red. Tammie was in the room with her, taking her stats. It was earlier than the usual visits, but she'd been sent in to see if Emily said anything about the previous day. The only thing she brought up was asking whether the video had been sent yet; something Tammie stated she didn't know. Other than that, all Emily asked was, 'How's James doing?'

Tammie lied, 'He's doing better now that he's in isolation.' She'd seen it before when subjects became violent. While she didn't know much about what Kiefel had done yesterday, in talking to James, she knew it never usually had a happy ending.

'That's good then.'

'It is,' Tammie said again as her mind circled back to what had happened before with the husband and wife subjects.

BEFORE

They should have seen the trouble coming; it had been quietly brewing just beneath the surface of "normality" with snide comments here and there between the imprisoned husband and wife, Mark and Sophia. Silly little comments: each of them seemingly looking to pick a fight at any given opportunity; born from the frustration and confusion of the situation they found themselves in.

Sometimes one would make a comment, and the other would ignore it. Then they'd stay in their room, as if they had any other choice, and sit in silence - neither one of them wishing to break the stale-mate. Other times, when one would pass an unkind comment, the other would snap straight back as the situation became a blame game. Their conversations would start at a normal level and gradually build until they were screaming at one another. The biggest problem being that, in these occasions, neither one was able to retreat to another room. They were literally stuck together.

On their last day together, the morning started like any other since being in the room. They'd stirred from the little sleep they had managed to get; they moved to their corner of the room when the white light turned red. They stood, dutiful, while one of the nurses' checked their stats. When breakfast was brought to them, they ate in silence – neither of them having anything to say to the other. Another problem with being confined to the same room, with nothing to distract them, being that conversation would dry up. There was only so many times they had ask how the other had slept, only so many times they could say "badly" and only so many times they could stand at the mirror, begging for information as to why they were being kept there.

No one knew what kickstarted the fight. The first they realised there was a problem was when Sophia slapped Mark's face. For the briefest of moments, he stood there with a shocked look on his face. *The briefest of moments.* She turned her back on him and made her way across the room to her own side when he stormed over to her, spun her around and slapped her straight back. Sophia hit him back, a fist this time. He stumbled back, not because of the force of the punch but because of the shock.

Hall had said, 'It's a ploy to get us to go in there.' While the couple had been snappy with one another from time to time, it had never escalated into physical violence. In her head, she presumed they'd missed a secret plan to cause a distraction which would get people running in. From there, she expected them to stop fighting and try and run - not that they would have got very far.

Except it wasn't an escape attempt. The sudden violence was a side-effect of the serum, unseen in previous experiments up until now.

Mark spat at his wife; a frothy mix of black goo which hit her directly in the face. She flinched and raised her bruised hand up to wipe it away and - still the doctors did nothing but watch, curious as to how far they'd go.

Hall continued, 'We can't trust them.' This time, she sounded like she was trying to convince herself more than anyone else.

Henderson suggested, 'We should call Dr. Kiefel.'

'And have her think we can't handle this? You know what they're like here. The moment they think we can't do something, we're reassigned… Do you want to end up in the cooking room because I sure as hell don't.' Neither did Henderson. 'I'm telling you, when they realise we're not biting, they'll stop.' She turned her attention back to the viewing area and frowned. 'Didn't she hit him on the side of the head?' Both of Mark's nostrils were bleeding black. So were Sophia's.

Henderson had noticed too. 'I don't think they're acting…' She'd barely finished the sentence when Sophia started thrashing her arms round wildly while stumbling around. No words came from her distorted mouth, only grunts and growls. Her eyes had started bleeding black too. 'Hit the alarm,' Henderson said. Hall didn't register her words. She repeated herself, louder this time, 'Hit the fucking alarm.'

Chapter Thirty-seven

Dr. Schwartz paced outside Sam's office while waiting for her to arrive at work for her shift. She'd been wrestling with her thoughts all night, tossing and turning in bed trying to decide the best way forward. She knew why Lucas was working as a guard and knew it was only a matter of time before he revealed whatever secrets he could dig out. When he did, it would cause trouble for the corporation, but that "trouble" would also spill over to those who worked there, including herself.

While there was a small part of her which thought it would be best to ignore it, that they were already suspicious of him, there was another voice in the forefront of her mind stating there'd be a fair amount to gain from warning Sam of his true intentions. The only reason she battled the idea of coming forward with the information she knew was that it would also come with questions. For instance, how does she know so much about the group? What if Lucas rolled over on the others within his circle and led Sam's legal team straight to Glynn? There was nothing stopping Glynn from showing he'd been in communication with her, before she changed departments, and how the original plan was for her to feed them all the information they needed to bring everyone down.

One way around it, she figured, was to deny everything. Most of the communications had been done via the telephone as opposed to sending text messages so there wasn't a paper trail to speak of. He *could* technically show he had her number and that there'd been a couple of calls between their phones but - a long shot - she could leave her phone at home and say it had been stolen. The fact the thief was part of the group? Nothing but a coincidence. Except, and herein was the problem, how convincing was that as an explanation?

Another way of explaining the calls was that she tried to infiltrate the group so as to gleam as much information about those involved. Information she would then pass over to Sam, once she had enough. Given everything had been verbal, it would be her word against theirs. If it came down to *that*, at least she'd be able to turn it against them by saying, 'If I was working to help them, why would I say anything about Lucas? Why not just leave him to carry on working here too?' But then, what if Sam decided the best course of action was to get rid of them both? That by stepping forward, all she was doing was putting a spotlight on herself - and one that's *not* positive.

'Are you here to find out about yesterday's meeting?' Sam's voice startled Dr. Schwartz and pulled her from her mental back and forth. Given how Jackie had been put on that experiment by Kiefel, it made sense Sam would jump to such a conclusion. Before Dr. Schwarz could answer, Sam continued, 'Once we know the outcome we will be sending out an email. But, the good news is, the meeting went well, and he seemed suitably impressed.' Even if Henry Phillips had already called through with his thoughts on the project, that was as much information as Sam would have given regardless. Schwartz was one of the doctors and her job didn't involve being "in the know" as to what was happening behind the scenes.

'Actually, it's not about that,' Schwartz said.

'Oh? In that case, to what do I owe this unexpected visit?' Her office phone started to ring from within her office; a loud, shrill ring which could be heard the entire length of the corridor leading from lift to office. 'Hold that thought.' She used her keycard to unlock the door and hurried over to her desk, dropping her shoulder bag on one of the chairs on the way.

Schwartz hovered in the doorway, unsure whether she was supposed to follow Sam in or not.

'Hello?'

Chmielewski was on the other end of the line. 'This is Dr. Chmielewski,' she said. 'I was wondering if I could have some advice, please? I've been trying Dr. Howard but she's still not in yet and I'm not sure how best to proceed.'

'You could start by telling me what this is about,' Sam said. She hated it when people dilly-dallied. Life was short, she just wanted them to get to the point.

'It's about the patient Dr. Kiefel spoke to yesterday. He's saying he wants to talk to her. I know Dr. Howard is the lead manager now so…'

Sam cut her off and said, 'I'll come down.' There were no goodbyes or other pleasantries, she simply put the phone down. She turned to head downstairs and stopped at the sight of Dr. Schwartz standing there. 'Well? What is it?'

Aware Sam was busy and already looking stressed, Jackie cut straight to the chase and said, 'Lucas Wilson is part of a group looking to sabotage what you do here.' With how quickly the words came from her mouth, she could tell they blindsided Sam. 'I recognised him yesterday. I've frequently seen him outside with the other protestors and just thought you should know.'

Unsure what else to say, Sam simply said, 'Thank you for bringing it to my attention.'

'I thought it was for the best.'

'Was there anything else?'

'What do you think you'll do about it?'

Sam frowned. Dr. Schwartz should have known better than to ask such a question. Even if Sam *had* known what "she was going to do about", it was none of Schwartz's business. 'That'll be all,' Sam said.

Jackie took the hint. Sam pushed past her and made her way down the corridor towards the elevator. Jackie hesitated a moment;

unsure whether she should let her go down by herself or follow in awkward silence. She chose the latter and pretty much regretted the decision the moment they both stepped into the lift and the doors closed. She couldn't help but wonder that, maybe, it might have been a little better had there been some music or something. A possible suggestion for any *Make it Better* surveys they might put out to staff.

Chapter Thirty-eight

'So, the other lady, Kiefel, told me I'm an experiment. That the real me is dead. Even showed me videos of how we're made and what happened last time my DNA was used in one of these test things,' James said to Sam.

Sam was standing by the main door. The guard from outside was with her to ensure the "patient" didn't try anything stupid. To ensure privacy was maintained, she'd cleared the viewing room and forbidden anyone to return until she gave them the go ahead.

James continued, 'She said I have a choice as to how to proceed. Apparently you're more than happy to start again. Farm some more of my DNA and go from scratch or, if I am willing to accept things as they are, you can make my time here more comfortable.'

Sam bit her tongue. This was a deal Dr. Kiefel had apparently offered but it wasn't one which had been signed off if he *had* chosen to have a more comfortable lifestyle. The main reason it hadn't been signed off being - it *wouldn't* be accepted. Not when it would end up costing more unnecessary expense. She let James continue.

'But what if there's another way we can move forward and carry on working together?' He paused, half-expecting Sam to ask what his idea was. When she didn't say anything, he pushed forward with *his* solution to all of this. 'You still have the other woman… The one who was in the room with me when I first woke up. You don't need both of us here. So, I was thinking, you could let me out.'

Sam didn't mean to laugh but couldn't help herself. Of all the things she was bracing herself to hear, this hadn't been what she'd been expecting. Just as fast as the laugh escaped her mouth, she promptly swallowed it back down again with a half-arsed, 'Sorry about that.'

'You're going to want to see if people on the outside world can tell the difference between real people and clones, right? What better time to try that then now? I realise I can't go back to my old life because, as the other doctor said, I'm dead now but what if you set me up someplace? I could wear a tracker or something, report in daily with progress updates. You could even get me here each day doing admin or something… The most important thing is that I'm *out there* though, mixing with *real* people… Because I take it the whole point of this is you're making us *not* to stand out… To blend in with the normal people.' He paused, waiting for Sam to step in with something to say. When she didn't he asked her directly, 'Are you going to say anything?'

'I've just walked into the room. That's quite a lot of information you've thrown at me,' she said.

'And, if you stop to think about it, it makes sense.'

'It does,' she said. 'It made sense the first time you said it too.'

James hesitated. 'What?'

Sam walked over to the bed on the other side of the room, putting distance between them, and took a seat on the bed's edge. 'We have been here…

* * * * *

…BEFORE.'

James watched in horror as Emily violently thrashed around on the bed with black vomit coughing up from her oesophagus. Unsure what else to do, he turned and hit his hands against the mirror. 'We need help in here.' He needn't have bothered. The viewing staff had already raised the alarm and "help" was already on the way.

The door swung open and Dr. Chappo hurried in with a guard by his side. Such was the suddenness of the situation, they'd not bothered switching the light to red, forcing James to stand in his corner. Despite the door being left wide open, he didn't make any attempt to run for freedom, such was his concern for Emily.

He said, 'She's having a seizure. One minute we were talking about the menus and the next…' Before he finished the sentence, Dr. Chappo gave a nod to the guard who instinctively knew what to do. The guard pulled his gun out and put it to Emily's head before squeezing the trigger. As her black brain matter decorated the white wall, James turned with a shocked scream, 'What are you doing?!'

Dr. Chappo gave a second nod towards the guard, not for instruction but - rather - an unspoken "congratulations" for a job well done. He turned to James who'd moved to the corner of the room in a desperate attempt to find some safety. 'I'm terribly sorry you had to see that. Rest assured we will be getting someone in here to clean the mess up just as soon as someone is available to do so.'

'You killed her?! You fucking *killed* her?! Who the fuck are you people?'

Dr. Chappo smiled. 'We didn't kill her. She was already dead many hours prior to finding herself here,' he said; a statement which only served to cause more confusion.

'What the hell is even happening?! What *is* this place?!'

It was always awkward when one of the tests failed before the other did. Such situations only served to raise more questions and general angst which, in turn, tended to speed up the process in which the serum failed. Watching James's stress levels reach a new high, Chappo was surprised he'd not already started to fit too. Still, he knew it was only a matter of time; clearly the serum was far from being perfected.

* * * * *

'She showed me footage where we smashed our bowls and went to cut ourselves,' James said. 'A failed experiment she said because of how we handled the situation… No one ever told me about any other times…'

Sam laughed. 'Do you honestly think we haven't used your DNA time and time again? You and Emily were amongst the first batch of DNA used. Even now we have more of you *cooking* because when the inevitable day comes we need to rush through another test. And, on one of those occasions, you were told the truth about the situation by one of the other doctors. The only difference between now and then - Dr. Kiefel had no authorisation to speak to you although, in fairness to her, she wasn't aware of the previous time the truth had been disclosed. She simply took it upon herself, thinking outside of the box, to try and fix a bad situation. Anyway, the last time you made the suggestion that it would be a good idea if you were free to, as you put it then, mingle with the real people out in the real world… Do you know what happened?'

James could hazard a guess. In his head, he could picture them answering with nothing more than a bullet and *that* was the real reason the guard had come in this time. His gazed turn to the man's side-arm.

Sam also turned her attention to the guard. 'Gun.' She held her hand out. The guard dutifully pulled his firearm and handed it towards Sam. The moment he released his grip, she turned the barrel towards him and squeezed the trigger, putting two bullets into his chest, before he had a chance to react. The guard dropped to the floor: Dead. At the sound of the first shot, James had turned his back to both Sam and the guard, half-expecting to feel a bullet penetrate his spine next. 'It's okay,' she said. 'I'm not going to shoot you. Turn around.'

Slowly, filled with uncertainty about how this would play out, James turned around as instructed. Sam pointed to the dead guard. Specifically, his chest. The two bullet-holes were leaking a white fluid.

Sam said, 'You've already helped us out in the real world. In fact, a version of you is still out there. Scotland, if memory serves me correctly although, while I doubt it, I could be wrong. New name, now *that* I cannot remember, new job…' She laughed. 'I don't recall exactly what he is doing but I do know he's actually earning more money than what you earned when you were alive working within that financial institution. That *did* amuse me.'

'But how would I not have knowledge of this?'

'Because once made, the clones react differently to their environments. Sometimes they go off the rails, sometimes they died from whatever serum we were testing on them and other times - like you now - they went the distance while we continued trying to perfect things. All clones start with the core memory of who they were before they died though so, why *would* you have knowledge about what happened to the other versions of you? Anyway, you should be happy… A version of you *did* help us take the experiment to the next level and to see that, yes, our clones could fit into normal society unknown.' She laughed for a second time. 'How many times have you heard someone say something like, *that person could have been your doppelgänger*? Sometimes it could just be that two people bear a striking resemblance and other times… You never know… Could actually be a clone.' She nodded towards the guard. 'Like our friend here. And don't worry about him either, he's part of our DNA database so we have spares.' She smiled. 'We have spares of all our staff. Part of getting a job here is to go through a medical and during that time, we do indeed take blood.' She added, 'That's not to say we don't occasionally bring in fresh blood but that's more for the database than because we *actually* need them… But anyway, that's by the by. The point is, we have no need to send you out there. While Dr. Kiefel had no right to tell you the truth, she did give you your two options and those remain on the table.'

'But if you know the clones work out in the real world, why do you need to keep us here? Surely you have everything you need?'

For the second time, Sam pointed to the blood. 'Because the blood isn't right. Every day, whenever we feed you your meals, we're trying different things to turn the blood the correct colour. We *need* to have it running red. We need to make *you* so if something were to become of you, out in the real world, there wouldn't be a million and one questions as to why you bleed white.'

James glanced at the door. It was open a fraction; purposefully left like that so Sam could get out again given the fact she'd already known she was going to shoot the guard. With a sudden burst of adrenaline, he lunged for the opening.

Sam fired two more shots.

Part Nine
The show goes on

Chapter Thirty-nine

Only Dr. Chmielewski knew what had happened in the white room; all other staff had been kept away until the clean-up operation had been completed. It was easier that way as it meant Sam didn't need to think of an excuse as to how the guard had been killed. Chmielewski was one of the handful of staff members who already knew he was one of the many clones working within the building, oblivious to the fact that he also was a clone. She *didn't* know some of the clones had been released into the real world. As far as she was concerned, everything was contained within the complex while they were working on getting the blood to run red.

Dr. Kiefel was shocked to hear that Sam had terminated James's experiment. While she knew Sam was angry with her for telling him the truth of his situation, she didn't think she would have so easily pulled the plug on it. Sam's excuse, not that she needed one, was that he'd turned unnecessarily aggressive and wouldn't be controllable. She put the blame solely on Kiefel's shoulders, even going so far as to say she could have got him on side had she kept her mouth shut about the purpose of the experiment. *Another black mark to Kiefel's once impeccable record.* Despite her growing frustration and the obvious power struggle going on, Kiefel still kept her mouth shut, with Sam at least.

'You should have come to get me,' Kiefel said as they waited for the new test subjects to be wheeled into the now-clean white room. 'You knew I was waiting to talk to him.'

'And I also knew the trouble you got into for telling him everything,' Chmielewski fired straight back. She explained, 'The patient was calling for you, so I tried to get hold of Dr. Howard...'

'Dr. Howard? *I* was dealing with it.'

'And she's the line manager now. When I couldn't get her, I reached out to Sam to ask how she wanted to proceed; call you or wait for Dr. Howard and she chose to take care of it herself.'

'Yeah, well, she did a great job of that, didn't she?'

'She did what was necessary.'

'She set everything back to square one and you know it. How long has he been here? The longest running test yet and, because of you running off to Dr. Howard and Sam… Right back to the start we go.' Kiefel gave Chmielewski a slow round of applause as she sarcastically said, 'Well done. Nice going. What do you do for an encore?'

Chmielewski smiled. 'I guess my encore is saying Sam called you and asked you to go to the cooking room.'

Kiefel rolled her eyes. She didn't say as such, but it was clear what she was thinking, *Oh for fuck sake - now what?* Given they'd not long since had the conversation about James, she didn't know what the hell she could have wanted *now.* It also pissed Kiefel off that she'd wasted time talking to Chmielewski when she'd been sitting on the message. Sam hated it when people kept her waiting, it was common knowledge, and yet Chmielewski had *purposefully* taken her time in passing on the message. Unable to bite her tongue, she said, 'You're a fucking snake.'

'Wow. Nice. And, may I ask, why's that?'

'You know why.' This was just another example of how the staff here were more concerned about their own jobs within the company than being part of a team.

Knowing she didn't have the time to get into it now, Kiefel walked from the room just as Dr. Howard walked in, ready to start her twelve hour shift. The first thing she noticed was that the white room was empty on the other side of the viewing window. 'So, what did I miss then?'

As Kiefel continued down the corridor, she called back, 'I'm sure Dr. Chmielewski can fill you in once she's stopped stabbing people in the back.'

Confused, Dr. Howard turned to Chmielewski who just shook her head in disbelief. Meanwhile, in the room behind them, the door opened. A guard, the same one shot dead by Sam earlier that morning, wheeled the first of two beds in along with another staff-member. James was on the first bed, Emily was on the second.

* * * * *

James watched from across the room. Emily was sleeping soundly; quiet little snores which brought him some comfort despite his predicament. *Naked*, just as he was.

It took everything not to call across and wake her. The only reason he didn't being that, with her sleeping, he was safe from whatever *this* was. Was she a part of it? Was it her who, somehow, brought him to this room? Was she the one who had removed his clothes and hidden them. No. Ridiculous. It couldn't have been her. At least, certainly not by herself.

Chapter Forty

Dr. Kiefel turned into the cooking room and stopped in her tracks at the sight of her body lying on one of the tables. 'What's this?'

'This,' Sam explained, 'is me making an executive decision; one which, truthfully, should have been made before when you first started losing focus…'

'Losing focus? How did I lose focus? You might not agree with how I handled yesterday but it was the best option I had to save us from needing to start again. So, what now? You're going to wake *this* up to carry on working here? How? It won't have all the memories I have *from* working here - just the memories from before, when you made us take the medical. I'm presuming that's when you got the DNA sample anyway? Pretty sure that's illegal.'

Sam laughed. 'And I am pretty sure a lot of things we do here are illegal. And, yes, it won't have your experience of working here but it will have your experience in the medical field and - we can re-train it; start it back from square one in an entry-level position.'

'You won't get away with this.'

'But we will. And, for some time now, we already *have*. Your conversation with the patient yesterday. It's a conversation Dr. Chappo had long before you were put in your management position. Do you *know* how many clones we have out there already? Well, no, of course you don't.'

Kiefel had heard enough. She turned from the room and hurried down the corridor towards the elevator. Sam didn't chase. She didn't need to. The elevator doors opened before Kiefel reached them and two guards came out, both with guns in their hands. Two of the longest standing guards working there, they'd already been briefed on what was happening and knew how Sam operated. Kiefel stopped in her tracks. She slowly turned back around to see

Sam watching from the doorway to the cooking room, a smile on her sadistic face. She said, 'This is happening and tomorrow will be just another day. We'll carry on monitoring the clones we have out in the real world. We'll continue working on the formula here to get the bloods right... And no one will stand in our way; be it someone from the outside trying to bring us down or from within. We've all worked too hard to make this happen.'

'I can just leave. I can go and you'll never see me again. You've fired people before. We both have.'

'Yes. But your level of expertise is valuable to us and if we let you leave... Where will the clone live?'

'It'll just take over my life?'

'That's exactly what it will do. But without the baggage you've been carrying for these last few weeks.' Sam explained, 'It's just business.'

Kiefel was shoved from behind as a guard stepped forward and pushed her back down the corridor. In the next room down from where they cooked the bodies, they'd already prepared another room ready for what they needed to do next.

Sam momentarily changed the subject, 'You employed Mr. Lucas Wilson. Did you do so knowing he was working on the outside to bring us down? Or did you just not vet him properly?'

'I have no idea what you're talking about.'

'It's been brought to my attention he's one of the many protestors...'

'I didn't know.'

'So, you just didn't vet him properly. And you wonder why we find ourselves in this position today? It's all been leading up to this.'

The guard gave Kiefel another shove further down the corridor towards the last room she'd ever see. 'Keep walking.'

'The other staff will know I'm not me anymore though. You'll get them asking questions as to why I suddenly don't remember them…'

'Which is why you'll be put in one of our other offices where they *don't* know you. Did you forget from your induction we have offices all around the country? For example: Did you know Dr. Chappo works in the north office now? He's doing as much good up there as he did down here for us, right up until he was killed.'

'We can talk. We don't have to do this.'

'Yes. We do.' She looked to the guards beyond Kiefel and gave them a nod. Instead of pushing her to the room, they each grabbed an arm and forcefully dragged her the rest of the way despite her protests. When they passed Sam, she followed - keen to watch the termination take place for herself. In her head she didn't see it as murder. She saw it as putting down someone who'd clearly lost their way, giving them a chance to live again while simultaneously correcting any previous mistakes. As such there was no guilt associated with what was to happen.

The guards pushed Kiefel into the room. Unlike the other rooms, the walls here had been covered with white plastic sheeting. There was similar sheeting on the floor too. It was obvious as to why the room had been decked out in this fashion and only served to make Kiefel panic more. She said again, 'We don't have to do this.'

'It's for your own good just as much as it is for us,' Sam said.

The guards shoved Dr. Kiefel into the centre of the room. She immediately turned to face them. 'How do you sleep at night?' She knew there was little point in trying to sway Sam's mind now. All she could do was try and convince the guards what they were doing was wrong. From their expressions, she already knew her words would be wasted but she didn't care. If this was her time, she wasn't about to go down without trying to stop it from happening. 'Please I'm begging you, I have a family.'

Sam laughed. 'She doesn't. Although she does have cats.' Directing her conversation towards Kiefel, Sam reassured her, 'And I am sure the new you will look after them very well.' Then, she added, 'If anything you should be thanking me.'

'Thanking you? Why the hell would I thank you?'

'Because, currently, you're headed for unemployment. No money to pay the bills, no references to help you gain employment elsewhere. You'd be struggling to live comfortably, might even lose your home. Does that sound like a fun life? I don't think so. Here, now, you get to reset and the new you will be able to, hopefully, push on with more success.'

Dr. Kiefel said, 'I don't want to die.'

'And technically you won't.' Sam signalled the guards. They raised their rifles and, without the need of further instruction, emptied a full clip into Kiefel.

As the bullets riddled her body, she stayed standing. Each bullet hit rocked her body with one eating into her shoulder and spinning her on the spot allowing others to bury into her back and spine. Only once the firing stopped did her body drop to the plastic covered floor as her red blood dribbled down the surrounding walls. There was no need to check for a pulse.

'I'll leave you to clear away the mess,' Sam said.

The guards reloaded their rifles, so they were ready for whenever the need for them arose again. Happy with how everything had gone, Sam stepped from the room. A little further down the corridor, Dr. Kiefel was wheeled from the cooking room on one of the beds. From here, she'd be loaded into the back of a private ambulance and driven to her new place of work, away from the staff who'd realise something was amiss once they realised she was missing the more recent memories of what she'd been doing.

Sam called out, 'Did you do the finger-prick test?'

One of the medical staff nodded. 'Still not red.' Sam's moment of relief, for having this situation handled, was short-lived as frustration once again took ahold. The staff member noticed her disappointed look and reassured her, 'We have some other things to try and are fairly confident though so, watch this space.'

'Forgive me if I don't get my hopes up,' Sam said. She'd lost count of the number of times she'd heard something similar only to then be disappointed in the lack of progress. Still, that was tomorrow's problem. Today was all about putting out the fires and, as far as she knew, there was still one outstanding, immediate issue to deal with after she'd informed the other staff that Dr. Kiefel would not be returning.

Chapter Forty-one

Dr. Schwartz didn't have much to do. The secondary experiments were on hold now they knew the serum worked as it should; letting people live normally until they died and *then* hatching the creatures from within them. All she could do was sit at her desk and wait to be relocated to another department. That's what she hoped would happen anyway. There was a chance there weren't any other slots available for her to fill and if that was the case, she couldn't help but worry she'd be fired.

Her computer's speakers audibly pinged as a new email came through. A quick glance and she saw it was from Sam. Without reading the subject, she presumed it might be to do with a new role so quickly opened it. Her heart momentarily sank when she noticed it was a group email to all the medical staff. The sinking heart was only "momentary" once she started to read it. She smiled:

With immediate effect Dr. Mary Kiefel will no longer be working in these offices. She has gratefully accepted a new position in one of our offices up north. We wish her the best in her new role.

'Ding dong the witch is dead.'

But…

Jackie's smile was just as short-lived as her initial sinking feeling. With her role in these offices now at an end, what if Sam transferred her to the same office? What if she was *still* stuck with the bitch? Perhaps, she thought, that would be a time to cut her losses, hand in her notice and find another job elsewhere. Her train of thought was interrupted when another email came through, also from Sam. This wasn't a group email; it was a request for her to go to Sam's office. And, with thoughts of being transferred up north with Dr. Kiefel, *that* sinking feeling was back.

She emailed back to say she was on her way even though, in reality, she would have done *anything* to stall having to go up.

Henderson walked into the office to grab her lunch from the top drawer of her desk. She couldn't help but notice the look of thunder on Schwartz's face. 'How can you look so grumpy when you have nothing to do?' Henderson had come from a stint watching Emily. She would have been more than happy to swap places with Dr. Schwartz that morning. It would have made a welcome change to sit down and put her feet up for a couple of hours instead, surfing the internet while pretending to look busy.

'I've been summoned.'

'Sam?'

'Yep.'

'Okay. I was going to suggest we could swap places, but I think I'm good,' Henderson said.

'You seen the email yet?'

Henderson frowned. 'What email?' Instead of waiting for Schwartz to tell her, she woke her computer up. Sure enough there were a number of emails waiting - including one from Sam. 'What's this?' She read.

'I've got a bad feeling that I'm going to be relocated too. I saw that email and cannot begin to tell you how happy I was to see I wouldn't have to see Kiefel anymore. Then, just as I finished reading… Ping… Fucking email came through telling me to go up.'

'Ah.'

'I swear to God…'

'Maybe it won't be about that? Maybe she has something else lined up for you?'

'Doubtful.'

'I heard they put two new bodies in the end room. Maybe she'll put you in there with Dr. Chmielewski? From what I understand, they were happy with what you did in those other tests…'

Jackie sighed. 'Only one way to find out for sure.' She pushed herself away from her desk and stood. 'Just rip the band-aid off, right?'

Henderson tried to offer a reassuring smile. 'Well, good luck.'

'Thanks,' Schwartz said as she made her way towards the door that would take her to the elevator. She added, 'If I'm lucky a giant cartoon safe will drop on my head before I get there.'

Henderson laughed as she locked her computer and grabbed her lunch. 'I'm not sure of the likelihood of that happening, sorry.' She followed Schwartz from the room.

'Yeah, me neither.'

'I do think you'll be okay though,' Henderson said. 'Out of everyone here at the moment, you're probably in the best position. It's no secret Sam was fed up with Kiefel. She'd not delivered results for ages now and was replaced over it. Then, rumour has it, she told one of the subjects that they were just a clone of a person and… Well, you saw the email; now she's being transferred. You, though, have delivered what they asked you to. She'd be stupid to transfer you.'

'Yeah but that's not just a "me" thing is it. I just happened to be the doctor in charge of watching the test subjects and reporting my findings. The people who made it happen are the ones who kept working on the formula to get it right.'

'Well okay, yes, that's true *but* if Sam tries to give you credit - just take it.'

They reached the elevators. Schwartz hesitated, still not wanting to go up. Henderson pressed the call button instead and continued, 'Pretty sure she knows you and Kiefel don't get on too.'

'That's another thing! She might send me to the same office as further punishment to Dr. Kiefel.'

Henderson laughed. 'That would be funny, but I can't see it. Honestly, I think you're stressing over nothing.' The elevator doors opened and Henderson stepped in. Schwartz followed and pressed two buttons: one for the floor with the canteen for Henderson and one, straight up to the top floor and - Sam's office. The doors closed.

Another panicked thought raced through Schwartz's mind which she chose to keep to herself. What if this was nothing to do with her job and everything to do with what she'd told Sam about Lucas Wilson? The conversation had happened so quickly that there was every possibility Sam could have had more questions about that. Or she'd spoken to Lucas and he'd told her that - actually - *she* had also gone to the meetings and even offered to help smuggle information to them. As the thoughts circled in her stressed head, she felt her face flush.

The doors opened for Henderson's floor. 'I hope it goes well. Like I said, let me know.'

Half-joking and half-serious, Schwartz said, 'If you don't hear from me, tell my family I love them.'

Henderson laughed as the doors closed behind her.

Chapter Forty-two

Dr. Schwartz had her answer to what the meeting was about the moment Sam answered her tentative knock, asking her to 'Come in.' Her face immediately flushed at the sight of Lucas sitting opposite Sam, a concerned look on his face too.

'Thank you for coming,' Sam said. She gestured to the seat next to Lucas. While she wanted to turn and run, Jackie knew it would only prove whatever Lucas had told her. All she could do was take a seat and hope she could talk her way out of it. Sam had turned her attention back to Lucas. 'It's been quite a morning today,' Sam said. 'A day of *putting out fires*.' She watched Lucas for any micro-expressions he might have pulled. 'Do you know why you're here?'

Lucas shook his head. 'Can't say that I do.' But seeing Dr. Schwartz there, he *did* know and it made him feel deeply uncomfortable.

'You don't know why I might have called Dr. Schwartz in?'

Still playing dumb, Lucas shook his head again. 'I'm sorry but I really don't know what this is about.'

'Uh huh.' Sam turned to Dr. Schwartz, 'Did you want to tell me again how you knew Mr. Wilson?'

Really, Dr. Schwartz wanted nothing more than for the world to open her up and swallow her down, but she knew she couldn't stay silent. If she went back on her story now, it would have just looked suspicious - especially if *he* ended up saying something about *her* involvement with his group. 'I said I thought I recognised him as one of the protestors who like to congregate by the front gates.'

Lucas turned to her with a frown on his face; the actor playing the part of the "idiot" who had no idea what the other person was talking about. 'The protestors?'

Sam was watching Dr. Schwartz's awkwardness with interest. 'That's not what you said. You said you *did* see him…' She turned her attention back to Lucas. 'You had a tour before you started your duties yesterday. Tell me, truthfully, *what* did you say to Emily when you were alone in the room.'

'I already said, she wasn't sure what she was going to say in the message she was supposed to record.'

'What if I were to tell you we had microphones in that room? That, even if you had your back to the viewing mirror and spoke softly, we could still hear you once we played the audio back?'

Lucas swallowed hard unaware that Sam was calling his bluff.

She continued pushing him, 'You told her about the experiment, didn't you? It's okay. Don't be nervous. Only yesterday we had one of our doctors tell the person Emily had previously been paired with…'

'You did?'

'Yes. We don't keep it a secret forever. We tell them when they first wake up that it won't be long before we give them all the details about why they're there. Can't very well keep them locked up without telling them, can we?'

'I told her,' Lucas said. 'Yes. I told her. What you're doing is wrong.'

'In your eyes. So, you took the job here to what exactly? I mean, you might as well tell me because you're fired regardless. Were you going to run back to your little group and tell them about us?'

Lucas stood his ground. 'What you're doing is wrong and needs to be exposed.'

'I see.' Sam added, 'Don't you think your plan to expose us would have been easier had you just played the role of "guard" normally and *then* tried exposing us once you no longer worked here? Because, right now, you've put yourself in a rather awkward and, I'm guessing, embarrassing position.'

'Who's embarrassed?'

'I admire your tenacity.' Sam sat back in her chair. She folded her arms and got to the point, 'You got through the vetting process, which is somewhat disappointing. You know too much so we can't very well just let you leave, can we?'

Lucas laughed. 'You're going to imprison me? I think my friends might have some questions when I fail to go home.'

'Who said you won't be going home?' Sam asked, 'Remember when you took the job? What did we do? The very first thing we insisted on?' When she grew tired of waiting for the penny to drop, she said, 'The medical? When we took your blood? Remember that?'

Lucas's face dropped.

'*You* won't be going home but, at the same time, *you* will be.'

Lucas looked at Dr. Schwartz, the panic written all over his face. 'This is a joke, right?' She wouldn't even look at him. He turned back to Sam and said, 'She doesn't recognise me from the protest line. She recognises me because she came to one of our meetings. Told us she was going to bring us all the information we needed.'

'That's a lie,' Schwartz said. 'He's just trying to confuse the issue.' Despite the fact it was her who was lying, she was grateful her cheeks didn't burn bright.

'Nope. Just saying it how it is.'

Sam picked the phone up. She pressed the zero and, within a second, the line was answered. She spoke down the receiver, 'Send them up.'

Lucas frowned. 'Them? Who's "them"?'

'I've heard enough,' Sam said. 'My colleagues are going to come upstairs; they're going to take you away. They're going to put a bullet in the back of your head. Your life, as you know it now, will end today. Within a few days we'll have you fixed up though. Before the tour, before your spoke to one of our test subjects. I will transfer you to another office, away from the tests and you'll spend your days working for us but never finding anything other than a normal running business with absolutely nothing to hide. This, you'll tell your friends and they, in turn, will soon lose interest in us. Meanwhile we'll still be here working on whatever we choose to work on and - the world will continue spinning.'

From beyond the office door, further down the long corridor, the elevator *pinged* as the doors opened. Four guards stepped out and marched towards the office.

Sam continued, 'We've worked too long and hard to let someone like you get in our way. We're also very close to finishing all we set out to accomplish so… Mr. Wilson, it was a pleasure to make your acquaintance and I hope the next time we meet, you're less irritating.

The guards ended the room with their guns drawn, ready to be used. Lucas refused to even look at them, choosing - instead - to maintain eye contact with Sam. 'This is just a sick joke. You're just trying to scare me into staying quiet. Fine, if that's what you want to hear - I won't say anything to anyone.'

Sam smiled. 'I know you won't.'

One of the guards said, 'Get up.'

Lucas still didn't even look at him. 'Fuck you.'

'I said, get up.'

'I'm not going with you. Fuck off.' The guards didn't need to know. Two of them grabbed Lucas and, despite his best efforts to shake them off, pulled him up from his seat. 'Get your fucking hands off me.'

'If you're lucky, they'll make it quick.' Sam swivelled in her seat and looked out of the window as the dragged him away, kicking and screaming. She always liked the view out of the window, overlooking the dense forest out back. So peaceful and tranquil.

As Lucas's screams grew distant, Schwartz couldn't help but ask, 'Was any of that true? Are you going to kill him and then send a clone back to take his place?'

'What would you suggest we do with him?'

'What about if he has a seizure?'

Sam didn't bother to turn back to Schwartz. She was watching a bird nesting in a tree outside. She explained, 'The serum has been working fine for a while now. We just need to get the blood right...'

'You're sending Dr. Kiefel to a new location. Are you sending *Dr. Kiefel* to a new post?'

'A version of her who will hopefully perform better than the last.'

'You've cloned more staff?'

'We've cloned who we needed to.'

There was one burning question which was bothering Schwartz more than any of the others running through her mind. 'What about me?'

Sam slowly turned to face her. She smiled. 'We were impressed with how you performed in your last role. At present we're looking at options as where best to place you next but, rest assured, we will find something suitable *and* exciting for you. With regards to how you dealt with Mr. Wilson...'

'What he said - he was lying.'

'... I would like to thank you again for disclosing to me that you recognised him. Thank you. Other than that, what happened in here - that stays between you and me. Some staff know that clones already exist beyond this compound, others don't. I trust we can count on your discretion?'

Without hesitation, Dr. Schwartz said, 'Yes.'

'Good. That'll be all for now. You can go and take a break while I speak with Dr. Howard as to your new placement.' She smiled. 'You're part of *the* team now. Congratulations.'

Dr. Schwartz had been working there for a while now and thought she already was a part of the team but she didn't say anything. She simply smiled. Sam swivelled in her seat again, signalling the end of their conversation. Schwartz took the hint and promptly left the room.

Chapter Forty-three

Jackie walked into the cafeteria with her mind racing in all directions. She knew Sam had a nasty streak to her, but she didn't realise how vicious it was. She kept trying to tell herself that everything she'd said was nothing more than a lie to terrify Lucas into remaining quiet and that, when the guards took him away, they simply took him to the exit and let him go, maybe even warning him what *could* happen if he tried to say anything about what had happened. The problem was, she knew this was unlikely as, while many wouldn't believe him, there'd be nothing they could do if he *did* tell anyone. The news would already be out there before they'd have a chance to replace him.

It also terrified her that she'd also been subjected to a medical. What if they suddenly decided she'd become a liability too? What if she *had* believed what Lucas had told her about them knowing one another from the meeting she had attended? There were no texts or calls between Jackie and Lucas but what if they searched his phone and found messages to other people *discussing* the fact she'd been there? If such messages did exist, there'd be no way of talking her way out of it.

'Well?' Henderson had looked up from her book and seen Schwartz enter the room. From the look on Jackie's face, she presumed she'd not had the news she'd been hoping for. 'Are they transferring you?'

Pulled from her thoughts, Jackie tried to put her brave face on. She forced a smile. 'No. She said she was happy with how far I had come within the company. She's going to talk to Dr. Howard later about where to place me next, but she's made it clear I'm very much a part of the team.'

'Well that's great,' Henderson said.

‘And just goes to show they can be forgiving if you’ve made a mistake before. There’s hope for you yet,’ Jackie pretty much regretted the words the moment they came from her mouth as she realised they made her sound like an arrogant dick.

‘I mean I’m happy for you but I’ve not made a mistake and yet I haven’t had Sam tell me I’m a part of the team.’ She laughed as she got up and took her empty mug over to the washing bowl in the sink. She put it in the warm water and gave it a quick rinse around before letting out a little cry of pain, ‘Fuck!’

‘What’s the matter?’

‘Someone left a knife in here… I just cut…’ Her voice trailed off as she pulled her hand out of the bowl only to be confronted with white ooze coming from her wound. She frowned and quickly hid her hand from Dr. Schwartz.

‘Are you okay?’

* * * * *

BEFORE

The doors opened and the guards ran into the room with Mark and Sophia. They were closely followed by both Dr. Hall and Dr. Henderson. Whatever was happening to the once-husband-and-wife, this was entirely new.

The two “patients” turned to the door the moment it had opened with both hate and hunger in their eyes. They lunged forward, mouths open and ready to bite. The guards opened fire as both Hall and Henderson flinched with the sound of each shot. By the time it was over, Sam was standing in the doorway just behind them - a disappointed look on her face. She said, ‘Well I can’t pretend I’m not bitterly disappointed. I think it’s about time we had a little chat. Don’t you, ladies?’

* * * * *

TODAY

Henderson didn't know what was happening. She remembered getting the job, she recalled working in the cooking room before being transferred to watching Emily after they'd moved her and yet, from the sight of the white blood coming from her hand, there must have been more to her story here. Confused and scared, she hurried from the room as Schwartz called out for a second time, 'Are you okay?'

It was clear from Henderson's expression she wasn't okay. Curious about what could have upset Henderson so suddenly, Schwartz got up and made her way over to the sink. There was a cloud of white mixed into the washing up bowl. Her heart skipped a beat as she realised what it meant, and what Henderson had just come to learn about herself. She glanced back over her shoulder, unsure whether Henderson would make a reappearance. She didn't but thoughts of Henderson were quick to disappear from her own mind as another concern came to mind. Henderson hadn't realised she'd been replaced until now. What if…?

With her heart racing, Jackie reached into the washing-up bowl and picked up the very same knife Henderson had accidentally cut herself with. Her hand shaking, she put the point of the blade to her finger-tip and held it there a moment - unsure whether she was willing to accept a possible truth that such a pin-prick could reveal. But then, could she continue living knowing there was a *chance* she was no longer herself? Maybe it was better to be in-denial? Maybe it was better to just keep moving forward as though she were her normal, red-blooded self? No. She needed to know, otherwise the question would forever be hanging over her head.

She sucked in a lungful of air and held it there, steadying her nerves. She closed her eyes and, a brief pause, pressed the tip of the knife against her finger-tip with enough pressure to pierce the skin. She felt the warm blood run down her finger and put the knife down on the side. All she needed to do now was open her eyes and see what was running from her. Or rather, see what the colour was. White or red?

White or red?

White or red?

Slowly, cautiously and with a heavy sick feeling in the pit of her nervous stomach, she opened her eyes and glanced down…

End.

Printed in Dunstable, United Kingdom

79812421R00107